THE HOUSE stood on a high sloping mound. It was long, low, very solid, and much larger and more imposing than Rose had expected. It was half timbered and the boarding was white, the great oak cross-beams black. It had the most enormous roof she had ever seen on any house. It hung over the upper storey windows like eyebrows meeting . . .

And all around Endel was marsh, and dykes . . . dykes deep enough to swallow a tractor.

This was Endel, the family home, and Rose, visiting it for the first time, found herself stiff with apprehension, found she had to fight an urge to leave the house and return to London . . . And when she met David Lofthouse her fear and apprehension grew . . .

Also by Lucilla Andrews

and published by Corgi Books

Lucilla Andrews
writing as Joanna Marcus

A Few Days in Endel

CORGI BOOKS
A DIVISION OF TRANSWORLD PUBLISHERS LTD

A FEW DAYS IN ENDEL
A CORGI BOOK 0 552 11429 4

Originally published in Great Britain
by Barrie and Jenkins Ltd.

PRINTING HISTORY
Barrie and Jenkins edition published 1978
Corgi edition published 1980

This book is set in Linotype Times

Corgi Books are published by Transworld Publishers Ltd.,
Century House, 61-63 Uxbridge Road,
Ealing, London, W.5.
Made and printed in Great Britain by
William Collins Sons & Co Ltd, Glasgow

CHAPTER ONE

He was standing behind me in the queue waiting to buy chair-lift tickets at the foot of the Alterberg that morning. He was the right tallish, sturdy build of a good skier and he wore the black quilted anorak with a mandarin collar and heavily rimmed black glasses that were uniform for trendy German skiers that winter. He had on a bright yellow tea-cosy hat, the flaxen hair at his temples was bleached white and he was chatting-up a large blonde Berliner in baby blue. I had seen her on the slopes in the last week. I had never seen him before. I would have remembered as beneath the tea-cosy and behind those glasses, he could have been Charles. I would have remembered as I was Charles' widow.

I propped my skis against the booth to buy my tickets. When I turned for them Yellow Hat handed them to me with a correct little bow. I said, 'Shönen Dank', and he said, 'Bitteschön, Fraulein', and returned his attention to his blonde. That suited me as I had nearly reached the limit of my German vocabulary and raising ghosts was not my favourite pastime.

The lift attendant wrapped a blanket round my waist and half lifted, half threw me into a moving chair. Yellow Hat swung upwards in the chair behind me. He was wearing his skis and sitting back, as the old hands did, with his legs crossed and without bothering to fix the safety chain. My skis were clipped together and lying across my chair-arms, so I did not notice the screw in the left toe-clip working itself loose and dropping out. It had to have happened then as the screw had been there when I skied down from the Classes Meeting Place to the foot of the lift.

I discovered it had gone directly I got on my skis at the top. Luggi, my class instructor, sent me straight down.

5

Luggi said he wished his class alive to stay and proper repairs must at the ski shop only be made.

Ernst, the ski mechanic at the shop, was very dark and half Italian. 'Is lucky she come out on the lift and not when you make the run down. Today the snow is fast, no?'

'So Luggi says. He thinks I might easily have broken something.'

'Ach, so!' Ernst beamed. 'Very possible!'

My hotel was roughly three hundred yards above the village. Walking back up the narrow snow-packed road, I watched the line of dots that was my class following Luggi's transverse run down. A black dot topped with yellow streaked by them in a straight run. He was as good a skier as I had guessed from his build, and worth watching in action. I did not stop to watch.

Herr Schneller, the hall porter, was eating a dumpling stew in the little office beyond his desk. He did not hear me and choked on a bit of dumpling when he saw me waiting. 'So sorry, madame!' He bounded out and as we were mates his hand did not shake too much when he gave me my key and the one letter that had come for me in the mid-morning mail. 'No class, today?'

He crossed himself when I explained. He was a Tyrolean, in his fifties and an educated man. He had been a schoolmaster until he turned soldier. For the last twenty years the only job he had been able to hold down was his present one, and that because the hotel was owned by his brother-in-law. He was a pale grey man and thin as paper. He had a face like a skull.

Occasionally he talked of his war to me and always as if it had been fought exclusively between the Russians and the Germans. If anything, he hated the Germans the most, which made life tough for him in the winter sports' season. When life got too tough, Herr Schneller retired to his little office and wept over the fringed tablecloth. Once I had lent him a shoulder and given him a box of tissues. That was

6

one reason why we were mates. There were others. I never asked him about Stalingrad. He never asked me about my late husband.

My letter had an English stamp. The postmark was blurred and the handwriting strange. I didn't open it. During the last year I had acquired the habit of carrying my mail around unopened, sometimes for days. Curiosity was another emotion in which Charles had left me in short supply.

I went up to my room to get out of my outdoor clothes, but the maids were still in there cleaning. The one lounge was crowded, so I went out on the terrace. There was no sun that day so I had it to myself.

The terrace ran the length of the west side of the five-storey wooden building. It overlooked the village, the nursery slopes directly below and the Alterberg across the valley. Even without the sun it was sheltered as the overhang of the roof reached a point directly above the broad wooden balustrade. The roof edge was now fringed with long, thick, pointed icicles. The hotel guests considered those icicles the best barometer in the village. When the temperature rose a couple of degrees they shed slow heavy tears on to the backs of our necks as we leant on the rail. The wooden surface was dry when I leant on it and thought about my lost screw and Ernst's saying I was lucky.

A Spanish maid once said, 'The good are lucky, Señora.' On that occasion, I had had measles.

The Classes Meeting Place was beyond the first nursery slope. The scarlet posts carrying the ski instructors' names, were stuck in the snow and looked like streaks of blood. I wondered why I had not noticed that previously and then how the snow had looked on a French mountain a year ago. Charles had been returning to Spain from a trip to London to fix up a new series of articles with his agent. His aircraft had lost height in a storm and there had been no survivors. Had I not had that belated attack of measles, I

7

would have been with him. We had then been married two years. We had no children. People said, the pill, of course. I said, of course.

The lounge door opened behind me. My circulation did a stop–go as Yellow Hat gave me a rather less formal little bow. He sat in one of the wooden-painted chairs against the wall and opened a German newspaper as Lisa, one of our waitresses, followed him out with a glass of beer on a pewter tray. 'Bitte, mein Herr.'

He said something that made her squeal coyly, which was no problem as Lisa was a great squealer. As my German was so limited I couldn't be certain the conversation concerned me, until Yellow Hat hitched down his glasses and gave me that questioning smile that reads 'I'm willing, how about you?' in any language. I answered it by looking straight through him and if that meant one more vote against our joining the Common Market, there was nothing I could do about it. I thought of retreating to the lounge, but objected to being turned off my own terrace nearly as much as I objected to my own antipathy to his presence. I couldn't spend my life running away from fair men of a certain age and build and if he was German he would not try again now Lisa had almost certainly told him I was English. I remembered my letter. It would have to be read sometime. It might be good therapy now. I sat down and slit the envelope with the sidepiece of my dark glasses.

It was good therapy. I did not see Lisa leave and I forgot Yellow Hat. It was only after I had read the letter a third time that I was conscious of being watched. I glanced up and Yellow Hat bent a little too quickly over his newspaper. I made myself watch him, briefly. It was no use. I still wished to God he would go away. My letter had raised a row of unknown ghosts. I did not want another I recognized sitting right by me. I read the letter again and after a while, again I forgot Yellow Hat.

We were both still there when Adrian appeared with

two glasses of wine. 'Rose, my dear! I was simply gasping when I saw you through the lounge window!' Adrian widened his large brown eyes and raised his mobile eyebrows to the fringe of his brown beatle-cut. 'How come you're down?'

I told him. 'Why're you back early?'

'My dear, our class is kaput! Absolutely kaput! There are now only the two Masons and myself left and Koni wants to push us all into Heinz's lot! I refused! I simply refused! Heinz is a butcher and if his class's bones aren't going snap, crackle and pop all over the Alterberg, he doesn't think he's earning his lolly! Koni says I can join Luggi's tomorrow, but if you're catching them up this afternoon, I'll ask Koni if I can tag along with you.'

'That'll be fun though you're much too good for us.'

'Think how that'll boost my ego.' He lowered his long thin body into the chair next to mine. 'And I'll be with you all day.'

I liked Adrian, affectations and all. He made me laugh. He had been my shadow since we met on the platform at Calais. I had been surrounded by shrugging porters, with my luggage apparently lost for ever and the Calais–Innsbruck express due out in a few minutes. My French was fair. Adrian's was perfect. He had been educated in Switzerland and was tri-lingual in English, French and German. He had found my luggage, my seat on the train and exchanged his with a Dutch boy in my compartment before we were clear of Calais. He had managed partly through his linguistic talents and partly as he had been able to pull a useful string. He had been at school with one of the couriers on the train.

His name was Adrian Browne. He had an Australian passport, but had not lived permanently in Australia since he was seven. His father had worked in Europe for years, but had now retired to Melbourne with his wife. Adrian was their only son. He was now in his last year at London University and reading economics. He said he had no rela-

9

tives in England and most of his friends were Swiss, but he adored London. At twenty-two, he was a year my junior, which gave him a tremendous kick and made life much easier for me as he was so easy to handle. He was sufficiently immature to get an extra kick out of my being a widow – which gave me an extra reason for liking him. Most people when confronted by a young widow feel uncomfortable and vaguely guilty, and it shows. Frequently, since Charles' death, I had been tempted to lie out of public spiritedness. I didn't have to, with Adrian. I could talk to him as I had not talked to anyone since I was first married. Naturally, though he liked my being widowed, he did not want to hear about my marriage, so I did not have to bore him or hurt myself.

I told him now about my letter. 'Read it. I'd like an outside opinion.'

'New job?'

'An invitation to a family reunion.'

'Family?' He accepted the letter, frowning. 'You said you hadn't any!'

'Nor have I, apart from these cousins I've yet to meet. Charles had none, as I told you on the train out.'

'So you did.' He read the letter, then looked up. 'This bloke Robert Endel? He's your cousin?'

'Yes. First cousin. The June he mentioned as his wife I've never heard of till now.'

'You'd heard of Cousin Robert? And this grandfather who died in his sleep last August? You must've!'

'Only vaguely. I knew my father had a father alive when he himself died. I knew he had an elder brother, Richard. I knew Richard Endel married a French girl who died in childbirth and that the child was a boy. I never knew his name till now. I never realized my grandfather was alive up to last summer. I knew Richard Endel was dead. He was killed in Normandy in 1944 the year after my father was killed in the Navy. Obviously, I don't remember him.'

'Did Grandfather raise young Robert?'

'I guess so.

'Only guess?'

'That's all I can do. Mother never talked about the Endels. I don't think she knew much. She never met 'em. When I was about seventeen she told me father had broken away from his family long before she met him and would never discuss them, even with her.'

He looked at the letter. 'Cousin Robert blames some blood row, but he doesn't seem to know what it was all about. Do you?'

'No.'

'Didn't your mother tell you?'

'I'm not even sure she knew. Like I've said, she seldom mentioned the Endels. After my father's death, we went back to her old home in Devon. We'd no relatives on her side left, but she'd lots of old friends. We lived there till she remarried when I was sixteen and we moved to London. We were living in London when mother and my stepfather died in a car crash just after I first met Charles. He helped me through all that had to be done. I didn't let the Endels know. Never dawned on me that I should. I've never missed them. I can't imagine why Robert Endel now wants to meet me.'

'Couldn't it be like he says? That as you two are, at the moment, the end of the line, he'd like to get together? Why not take him up? Spend a few days in Endel, like the man says.' The rustle of a newspaper made him glance round. He jerked a thumb. 'What's he?'

'I think, Deutschlander.'

Adrian had another look. 'Could be. Right clobber. He speak English?'

'Search me. Adrian, should I accept this?'

'What've you got to lose? If you like 'em, could be fun. If you hate their guts – well, so what on a long weekend?'

'You may be right.'

A maid on the fourth floor shook out a rug and we both looked up. The fringe of icicles jangled but held firm. The dust particles floated down slowly on the still, frozen air. I watched one speck and made a bargain with myself. If it went over the balustrade, I'd say, no. If it landed on the terrace, I'd accept.

Adrian asked, 'What kind of a joint is this Endel House? Old?'

'Very, if it's the one in which my father was born. He was in the fifteenth generation in the direct line to do that.'

'He was? Rose! This you must see!'

'Why?'

'My dear! Where's your sense of history? Your family pride?'

'Don't possess either.' My speck was dithering in mid-air.

Adrian re-read the letter. 'This bloke sounds decent. He says he's wanted to know you for years and has been trying to trace you since the old man died?'

'Nice of him. But why wait till then?'

'Maybe your being your father's daughter kind of stuck in Grandpappy's throat?'

'Maybe.'

'And Cousin Whatsit only managed to get in touch with your old headmistress who put him on to the girl with whom you share a flat in town last week.'

'So he says.'

He lowered the letter. 'Rosie, what's eating you?'

My speck had settled on the terrace without convincing me. 'I'm not sure I dig family reunions. Or perhaps I'm more my father's daughter than I ever realized.'

'Stuff that!' he said impatiently. 'Which century are you living in? What the hell does a row between three men all now dead matter now?'

I did not answer at once. I was thinking of Charles. He would have dropped Robert Endel's letter into the nearest dustbin. Mentally, I could hear his clipped voice. 'Only fools forgive and forget. I've never done either.'

I got up and leant on the wooden rail. 'You've got something there, Adrian. Let me think. I've another week here, so if I write today there should be time for a reply before I leave. As I'll be in England by Thursday of next week, if I went straight to Endel House for the weekend it might work out better than leaving it till later as I must get another job and no new boss'll enjoy being asked to give me a Friday to Monday free in my first couple of months as his secretary.'

'That's not a bad idea.' He joined me at the rail. 'As you're unemployed you could stay till Tuesday or Wednesday.'

'I think Tuesday morning at the latest from their angle as well as mine. By Monday night most weekend visits get stale.'

'You'll let your secretarial agency know?'

'There's no need. I'll ring 'em when I get back to London on the Tuesday. They always have so many jobs on their lists that I'll probably be fixed up by Wednesday. If I go to Endel I'll send a card to Jill at the flat telling her to expect me when she sees me, and – oh yes!' I smiled. 'I'll write to Mrs Kitz. She'll be dead pleased!'

'Who's this Mrs Kitz?'

'My last boss's wife. Didn't I tell you I've been working for an aged American who needed so much overtime that I saved enough for this holiday in three months?'

'Sure. You said he'd gone back to the States.'

'He has. To Detroit, Illinois, plus Mrs Thomas B. Kitz. She was a sweet old bag and got in a fearful tiz at my lack of kinfolk. Her glasses misted up every time she came into the office. She lost three rhinestones polishing them. I promised I'd keep in touch. I sent her a card the other day. I'll write her all – if I ever get to Endel House.'

He asked, 'Why the big if? Going to change your mind?'

'I don't think so. I may brood on it a little longer.'

'My dear, now why – ?' He broke off as Lisa appeared and reeled off a spate of German. 'Hell! I'm wanted on the phone. Coming in to join the beery throng, or will you finish your brooding out here? I'll be right back.'

13

'Then I'll wait here.' I had noticed Yellow Hat folding his newspaper. I did not look round when he followed Adrian and Lisa into the lounge, but was then so relieved to have the terrace to myself that I interrupted my brooding to give myself a sharp pep-talk. Either I took a grip, or I would soon find myself in a psychiatric ward. Perhaps this family reunion would be as good a therapy as that letter. It might be interesting to see the house and meet the Endels. It might even be amusing. I loved the country far more than I loved London, but I had returned to the latter as I had too many old friends in Devon. No one in London bothered to ask more than superficial questions. Jill was a Londoner. We had met as first-year six-formers when I was transferred from King's Abbot Girls Grammar to one in London. We had got on well at school without knowing much about each other and in our last six months as flat-mates our relationship had not altered.

The nursery slopes cleared for lunch. The chairs moving up the Alterberg were empty. The swooping fly figures vanished. It was all very still. There was no traffic coming up from the village, no sound of running water from the frozen mountain streams and no birds sang. In the silence one could almost hear the swish of the earth's rotation and the voices of dead men.

The whiteness before me turned blue. The improbable picture-postcard blue of the Mediterranean in May. The rocks were black and encrusted with salt. Charles disturbed a baby octopus in a little rock pool, niggling it with the toe of his canvas shoe until it thrashed in fear and let out a defensive jet that changed the water to blue ink. Charles said, 'I need you, Rose. Do you understand, now, why I had to wait to tell you?'

We had been married a week and I loved him. So I had lied. 'Yes. I understand.'

I shuddered violently, reminded myself of the present and the temperature and moved away from the rail. As I moved, the icicle fell.

14

It was about five foot long, inches thick and it crashed on the exact spot I had just left. It shattered on impact. The tip and roughly ten inches of ice remained embedded in the wood and vibrating like a thrown knife. The rest crashed on to the terrace, littering it with chinks and splinters of ice. I expected the noise to empty the lounge. No one even looked out. They were making too much noise in there themselves.

I brushed off ice splinters and very nervously looked upwards. The glass fringe was transformed into a row of giant teeth with one ugly gap up front. Directly beneath the gap and on the top balcony, Yellow Hat was looking down at me. He did not call out and was gone immediately. The silence returned. There were no drips on the wooden rail and the smallest ice splinters were too cold to melt.

I sat down and gripped my hands to stop them shaking. It must be a coincidence. He wasn't responsible for his resemblance to Charles. It was crazy to imagine he had deliberately knocked off that icicle. It could have killed me. Why should he want to try and do that? If it came to that, why should anyone? Yet, why had it dropped?

Adrian provided the sensible answer when he got back from his phone call. 'Gravity. Obviously, it had a flaw. When the weight reached a certain point it had to fall kerplop.'

'That's all there's to it?'

'The logical explanation. What more do you want?'

'Logic's not my strong point. And this could be my second near-miss in one morning. Think there'll be a third?'

He gave me a long lecture on superstitions being for the birds, and the ignorant, under-privileged birds at that. He said he wouldn't have thought it of me and looked quite hurt. As to tell him about Yellow Hat would make him think me even more idiotic and I had no wish to wreck too many of his illusions, I kept it to myself. We went in for a drink, he told me he had seen Koni in our hall and was

15

officially in Luggi's class from this afternoon. 'I'll collect your skis from Ernst after lunch and we'll go up together. Stop looking jittery, my dear! Nothing, repeat, nothing else is going to make a third for you!'

He was right as far as my health was concerned. Nothing untoward occurred to it that afternoon or for the rest of my holiday. But on our first run down the Alterberg a couple of hours later, he was on deep soft snow when his right safety snap snapped. He lost a ski, misplaced his right knee cartilage and tore two tendons in his right leg. When Luggi and two other instructors carried him down on the blood-wagon, I saw Yellow Hat leaning on his ski-sticks and watching from across the slope. Then he pushed off and waited at the foot for the little procession. When I reached the village doctor's surgery ahead of my class, Luggi was coming out alone. He was very glum. 'Never such an accident to one of my class have I had! I speak with Ernst! That strap should have broken not!'

'Luggi, one moment – how bad is Mr Browne?'

It was then he gave me the medical details. 'To hospital the Herr Doktor says go he must.'

'For how long?'

'Some days. One week. Who knows? I speak with Ernst!'

'Hold on – is he still in the surgery?'

'Ach nein! The ambulance leaving was. It delays.'

My class had joined me. I looked all round. There was no sign of Yellow Hat.

I wrote to Robert Endel that evening, then went down to the hall to ask Herr Schneller to stamp and mail the letter for me.

'With pleasure, madame.' He sighed mournfully. 'Poor young Herr Browne. His luck is not so good, no?'

'I'm afraid not. I rang the hospital before supper. He'll be there for the rest of his holiday.'

'Ach, so! It happens many times to skiers.' He rootled in drawers for a stamp. 'You will be lonely. A pity your

16

friend from England was here so short a time and returns to London tomorrow.'

'My – whom do you mean, Herr Schneller?'

He was puzzled and in consequence looked near weeping. 'The Englishman from Liederau. He gave no name.'

'Liederau? Isn't that nearer Innsbruck?'

'Ach, so! He came over today to ski the Alterberg and take pictures, he said. Naturally, he came mainly to see you, but being English that he did not say! I gave permission for him to use our ski rack and to take his pictures from the top balcony. Thirty and thirty-one are empty until the English family Carter arrive tomorrow.'

I liked old Schneller. It took little to knock him off balance. I had to be careful. 'Do they overlook the terrace?'

'Indeed, yes! Two of our best rooms!'

I said, 'The view up there must be perfect. I hope he got good pictures.'

'Your friend did not tell you so?'

I said slowly, 'Well, actually, Herr Schneller, as I was rather occupied with Mr Browne, no one else had much of a chance to talk to me.' He nodded understandingly. 'I'm ashamed to admit I didn't really notice – at least – not much – who else was around. A man did come out on the terrace, and since you mention it, there was something vaguely familiar about him. A man in black and a yellow hat. That the one? Oh, dear! I thought he was a German. He spoke it so well.'

'He spoke freely, but his accent was not good. Very English. And you did not converse with him? Ach, madame! You should have taken pity on the poor man coming to see you!'

'He told you that?'

'But, yes! He described you well and gave your name when he enquired for you this morning. I sent him out to the terrace. He said you had – what is the English – ach, yes – mutual friends. He did not tell you?'

17

'No.'

He spread his hands. 'No doubt he formed the impression you did not wish to be disturbed from your conversation with Herr Browne.'

'Possibly. Or possibly,' I thought aloud, 'as he had something of the look of my husband about him, he may be some connection of whom I've never heard and may have decided that perhaps it wasn't tactful after all to remind me of things past.'

'It may be so, madame. But very English.' Herr Schneller sighed again. 'A Tyrolean who wished to speak with and perhaps offer sympathy to a pretty young lady would not so have wasted his last day.'

I said he was so right, paid him for the stamp and went back to my room. That mutual friends line was one of the oldest in the book. Yellow Hat could have got my name from his blonde Berliner. I knew hers. The village was small enough for most of the tourists to know each other by name as well as by sight after a couple of days. He had seen me waiting for tickets, which provided him with my description. Surely he must have been either some distant connection of Charles', or nothing worse than a man mildly on the make who had lost interest after seeing me with Adrian? There was no logical reason why I should connect him with that falling icicle or Adrian's accident.

Unfortunately, as I had told Adrian, logic has never been my strong point.

CHAPTER TWO

A porter on Astead station tucked my luggage under his arms. 'Taxi, miss?'

Astead was a market town with the nearest mainline station to Endel House. In the letter that had answered mine by return, Robert Endel had explained the house was twenty miles from Astead and that I might have difficulty in finding a taximan willing to drive the distance. 'If you ring Endel from the station,' he wrote, 'it will give me great pleasure to drive in to fetch you.'

My porter escorted me to the public telephone box in the booking hall and waited outside the box. I dialled the number three times in vain, then rang the exchange.

'Hold on, please, while I check, caller.' After a silence, the operator's voice returned. 'My supervisor says that line's been down since lunch. As there's been no gale, she reckons it's a swan.'

'You did say – a swan?'

'That's right, dear. Their big wings, see. Shocking the damage those swans do our lines down the marsh! They will fly into the wires. You'd think they'd learn. They never!'

I commiserated with her on the low IQ of swans, rang off and then asked my porter's advice.

'Endel House, eh?' He pushed up his new issue cap to scratch his head. 'Tidy step from here. Down St Martin's way, ain't it?'

'Somewhere outside St Martin's village, I believe. About twenty miles.'

'Reckon it's all of that.' He reloaded himself. 'There's not many as'll fancy driving that far, but old Bert'll fetch you out if his cab's in and it were ten minutes back. Old Bert knows the marsh like the back of his hand seeing he's a Coxden man.'

'Is Coxden a marsh village?'

'Nah. Last on the mainland.' He took me into the yard and whistled. 'You're in luck, miss. There's old Bert.'

Old Bert was a huge middle-aged man with a broad, red, fine-featured face, very blue eyes and very gold hair. He looked as if he should be wearing a Viking's helmet rather than a peaked driver's cap, but would only use a battle-axe in self-defence. 'I'll fetch you out, miss. Fifty bob the double. All right, then?' He had a slow broad-vowelled voice and before we drove off he switched on his dashboard transmitter. 'Bert Mercer, Sandra. Off down Midstreet. I'll be out an hour and maybe more.'

I waited until we were clear of the outskirts of Astead and on a new highway running downhill through open country. 'Driver, is Midstreet another name for St Martin's?'

'Oh, no, miss. Midstreet's a good six miles on from St Martin's.'

'But I thought Endel House was near St Martin's?'

'It'll be in the parish of St Martin's, but Endel were the Manor House down Midstreet long afore they set up the new parish boundaries.'

'I see. This Midstreet – is it another village?'

'It were. Gone now,' he added laconically.

'Gone? Derelict?'

'Nah. Gone,' he repeated. 'The sea come in and fetched it out.'

'The whole village?'

'All but Endel House and the church. St Mary's, Midstreet, that'll be.' He settled himself into a more comfortable position. 'There was this storm, see, and the sea-wall gave. Cruel bad it was, they say, and the best part of a week afore the sea went down and all that time the water was round Endel and the old church. They reclaimed the land and patched up the wall later, and they still calls that bit of wall the Midstreet Wall, but they never rebuilt the village. Reckon there weren't many left to build for.'

I felt rather sick. 'When did this happen?'

He took his time. 'Matter of seven hundred years back.'

'And Endel House still survives?'

'It weren't the Endel as they got there now as had the water round it, though they do say the old house stood more than its time after they dried it off. Didn't burn down till – let me see – it must've been when the first Queen Elizabeth were a young lady and they put up this present job.' He turned the car off the main road and into a narrow lane. 'They put on the new roof, later.'

'Recently?'

'Not that recent, miss, though it might seem so to old Endel. They got on the new roof when that King Charles come back from France to take over.'

'1660? And that's recent for Endel House?'

He glanced back. 'Stranger, you'll be, miss?'

I said, 'I've never been here before.'

'Then you'd not know as there's been Endels down this marsh long as the marsh been here and that they were long afore the Romans come.'

I was more interested than I had anticipated. I said truthfully, 'I'm afraid I know very little about the Endels or Endel House.'

'Well, miss,' said Bert, 'you come to the right place for learning, haven't you, then?'

We drove into a village of the type used to advertise Olde Englande in American magazines. It had a wide main street lined with bare chestnut trees and old pinkish-orange brick houses that leant against each other and seemed to have grown out of rather than been built on the land. The lawns in the small front gardens were swept clean of leaves, the apple and cherry trees were carefully pruned, the bare hedges neat. Several of the houses had thatched roofs and there was even a forge with a cone-shaped roof and inside a blazing fire. Outside the forge, a youth wearing a long leather apron over mechanic's overalls, was working on a tractor. He waved a spanner as we drove by. Bert jerked up a thumb in reply. 'Young Ken,' he explained. 'My brother Tom's eldest lad. Tom runs the forge.'

'Then this must be Coxden? Your village?'

'How do you come to know that, miss?'

'The porter told me.'

'Ah,' said Bert, 'Harry's an Astead man. Astead folk reckon Coxden's the back of beyond. They should live down the marsh proper, is what I says. Then they'd see. And you'll see the marsh coming up, sharpish, miss,' he added, 'once we get over the Ditch.'

The wide main street suddenly narrowed between over-hanging houses built in a curve beneath the walls of a vast grey church with a high square tower. Directly we passed the tower we were on a small stone bridge that crossed a wide dyke. The water was brown and ran softly as oil. 'The Marsh Ditch,' announced Bert. 'Now we're off the mainland.'

The land had opened out to the horizon. It was a greenish-yellow flat land, lacerated by the long brown slits of the dykes draining seawards. The road was built up and lined occasionally by stunted trees and more often by low thorn bushes burnt brown. The sea was invisible but omni-present in the smell of the air, the salt on my lips and the crying of thousands of wheeling sea-birds.

I looked out of the rear window. The long line of low green hills marked the northern edge of the marsh as plainly as a line drawn on a map. 'I suppose that was the old coastline?'

'That's right, miss. The sea come right up to Coxden, previous. Proper port it were, they say, until the tide took itself out one night and didn't never come back. So the marshmen got theirselves stuck in the mud and started building their sea-walls to keep the sea out. The sea didn't fancy that much, seemly, and it still don't. Half a chance and it'll be back.'

I looked all round very curiously. 'Many villages suffered like Midstreet?'

'Many a one – and more than the once. But that don't shift out the marsh folk. Once a marshman gets hisself stuck in, he don't get shifted out easy.'

I thought of my father. A born marshman yet he had shifted himself out. Would he have come back, had he lived? I wished with an urgency that surprised myself that I knew the answer.

Bert said, 'Being a stranger you'll not know what they says down here.'

'No?'

" 'I holds to my own and once I got a hold, it's my own." '

I thought of Charles. He hadn't been a marshman. He could have been, apparently. Then to take my mind off that one, I thought of my cousin Robert and wondered if it was natural or peculiar that he should have so highly developed a streak of family-feeling that had been lacking in the man who must have formed his character.

Occasionally we passed an isolated cottage or small farm. The buildings were of grey stone, they stood squat and solid, with small deepset windows and low overhanging windowless roofs in gardens that were small seas of mud. The fields looked boggy, the fodder stacks were shrouded in black tarpaulin fixed with strong ropes to large stakes driven into the land. The silent tractors and other farm machines were chained to anchors half buried in mud.

I said, 'Mud must be quite a problem here.'

'You never said a truer word, miss! Mud! Gawd! Get yourself in a skid on a bit of marsh mud and you'll be better off on oil!' He braked carefully as a brace of pheasant scampered across the lane ahead. 'One mistake here and you're in the water.'

The lane was lined by dykes filled with rushes. The rushes had orange feather tips. 'These dykes don't look deep. Are they?'

'Deep enough to swallow a tractor and none be any the wiser, specially this time of year with all the sheep moved up the hills on the mainland and the holiday visitors gone. I'd not like to tell you the times I've helped haul a van or a car out these dykes, but it'll be more than I've had Sunday dinners! Mind you, when it come to a tractor, there ain't nothing'll shift it out but another tractor an' if you're not real careful that'll go in too. There's nothing'll skid like a tractor once he gets out of control, see. Ever you're on a tractor in a skid, you wants to jump clear quick, or you'll

23

not do much jumping no more. Let a tractor go over on you, miss, and that's your lot! But I don't reckon tractor-driving's your line, miss?'

'No,' I said, and he gave me a paternal smile in the driving mirror.

The distant sound of the sea was changing to a low roar. As we drew nearer the coast, the marsh itself changed. There were no more stunted trees, only a handful of thorn bushes and the land was broken with patches of pebbled green rock, patches of sand, clusters of sea-pinks their faces brushed open by the rising wind and wide salt-water pools. As we reached the sea road six Canada geese flew inland over the high thick concrete wall. They flew in formation and their wings were black against the parchment sky. On one pool four swans circled, and a kestrel hovered almost stationary high over a dyke.

Bert jerked a thumb. 'This here is the start of the Mid-street Wall. The old village boundary used to come right up to this road. All that land over on your left now'll be Endel land. And just about the best land on the marsh long as they keep it drained proper.'

The fact that the Endels owned any land was news to me. I asked if he knew the extent of the property.

He said thoughtfully, 'The farm's not as big as it used to be, but I reckon as young Mr Endel'll have around six hundred acres. Maybe more. Good farmer he is, they say. Warm man. Proper chip off the old block, seemly.'

'You mean by that, his grandfather? The late Mr Endel?'

'Aye. As passed on last summer.' He had another glance at me in his mirror. 'I take it you'd not have known the old gentleman?'

'No. Did you?'

'I'd not say I knew him, miss. Knew of him, you might say. Liked to keep hisself to hisself, he did. And where's the harm in that is what I says. And he's gone, natural, in his sleep.'

'So I've been told.'

'Aye.' He grinned quickly. 'And there's been many a red face in these parts since, I reckon.'

'Oh? Why?' I asked curiously.

Bert said, 'You know how it is in these isolated parts, miss. Get some real queer notions in their heads, folks do, and there's no talking 'em out of 'em, neither. Now you take my old mate Biffer Gillon. Biffer's a St Martin's man, see,' he explained. 'And I got a quart of mild and bitter out of my old mate Biffer when I heard how the old' – he paused – 'old gentleman passed on.'

'Why was that?'

'I'll tell you, miss. There's been Gillons down St Martin's long as there's been Endels down Midstreet, see, so there's not much old Biffer don't know about the neighbours. "Mark my words," he'd say when we heard as the old 'un was poorly, "he'll not go yet. Stroke he may have had," he'd say, "but he'll be up yet. He'll go when his time come, but not natural under his own roof. No born Endel never gone in Endel nor never will." But old Mr Endel done it! Real put out was poor old Biffer, but he paid up with me quart!'

'How very interesting.' I thought of my father's death and then of Robert's father's. 'I wonder how that legend got started? I suppose from a series of perfectly explicable coincidences.' (Like icicles, missing screws and weak safety straps?)

'Just what I tells old Biffer. You know what he says?'

'Do tell me?'

'What causes the coincidence, he says. You tell me that, Bert, he says, and you'll be a wiser man than meself if you can. Like I said, miss. There's no shifting notions out of some folks heads.' He slowed the car to drive up a cinder road. 'It were the bit of wall just behind us now that gave in the storm that fetched away Midstreet. And there's Endel House up there now. Nice place, though I'd not fancy it much for a home seeing as I likes a bit of company from

25

the neighbours, though I'd not say no if they offered me Endel Farm. The farm buildings'll be those up there far behind the house. A good two mile off from the house, they'll be. The vans get round to it by the main road, this bit being private, see.' His thumb was in action again. The large sign he pointed out read; 'Endel House. Private road. Private visitors, only.'

The dark grey cinder road curved between dykes, over stone bridges and passed a small cottage entirely surrounded by dykes and approachable only by a very narrow moss-covered stone bridge. A few yards from the cottage were the main gates to Endel. They were huge, made of iron that was encrusted with rust and fixed open.

'They calls that End Cottage,' said Bert. 'Mr Endel lets it to holiday visitors. Must have a tenant now seeing there's smoke from the chimney.'

I had lost interest in the cottage and was looking at the house still roughly half a mile off at the end of the cinder road. I thought aloud. 'On its knees.'

Bert said it always put him in mind of a cat. 'You seen a cat crouching to spring on a bird, miss? Looks just like old Endel, don't it?'

'Yes. Just.'

The house stood on a high, sloping, strengthened mound. It was long, lowish, very solid, very much larger and more imposing than I had expected. It was half timbered and the boarding was white and the great oak cross-beams were black. In the fading afternoon light, the lower brickwork was a dark orange and the roof was black. It was the most enormous roof I had ever seen on any house and hung over the upper storey windows like eyebrows meeting.

Bert said, 'It's the weight what done it.'

'Done what?' I queried absently. I had suddenly realized the moment I had been postponing mentally since I answered Robert's first letter, had arrived before I had got round to facing how I was to deal with it.

26

'The weight of the roof,' he slowed the car for the last twenty-five yards, 'see how it's shoved the foundations deeper in that mound? That won't do 'em no good.'

I was far too rattled by the prospect of launching myself as a house guest on unknown cousins to remember, and much less to remind him, that as the foundations had stood the weight for three hundred years, there did not seem to be any wild cause for anxiety on their account.

He stopped the car beside an old mounting block at the foot of the stone steps leading up to the front door. The sight of that block stirred a long-forgotten memory. My mother had once told me my paternal grandmother had loved hunting, and been killed in a hunting accident when my father was fourteen. She must have hitched her horse to the old iron ring in the block. I looked hard at the ring and tried to make myself believe that as her granddaughter and my father's daughter I was on home territory. I didn't succeed.

Bert lifted out my cases and offered me a hand. 'Stiff, miss?'

I wasn't stiff with sitting; I was stiff with an acute attack of nervous apprehension. I was so jittery that I had to remind myself all that obviously ailed me was the anti-Endel fixation that was bound to have been implanted in my subconscious as a child by my mother's refusal to discuss my father's family. That got me out of the taxi, but did not stop my wishing I had the moral courage to tell Bert to replace my bags and drive back to Astead and the first London-bound train. Bert wouldn't mind. Kindness to dumb animals, children and idiot females was written all over him.

It was too late. The front door had opened. A smallish over-plump young woman with an auburn chrysanthemum cut stood momentarily poised on the top step. Then she squeaked, 'You must be Rose! Robert's missed you! He left for Astead about forty minutes ago when we found our line was down! I'm June, Robert's wife!' She cantered down the steps and puffed. 'Didn't you pass a blue estate car?'

'I'm sorry,' I said, 'I'm afraid I didn't notice.'

Bert said he had noticed, and we hadn't. He handed my cases over to a small elderly man in a green baize apron, accepted his fare, touched his cap. 'Much obliged, miss. 'Afternoon, all.'

June took both my hands. 'So you're Rose!'

'Yes.' I hoped my smile did not look as weak as it felt. 'Hallo, June.'

'You can't think how thrilled we both are to have you with us!'

'It's very sweet of you both to ask me.'

'We've wanted to meet you for ages!' That squeak was apparently her natural voice. 'Robert's longed to know you ever since he was a boy and we both felt so dreadful when we heard you'd lost your poor husband and didn't know how to get in touch with you to tell you so. We would have loved to have you come straight here then but – well – Grandfather was – well – Grandfather.' She had large rather expressionless pale blue eyes. She flapped her eyelashes girlishly. 'Men! Can you imagine anyone brooding on a silly quarrel for nearly thirty years? Not that Robert's like that,' she gushed on before I had to answer, 'and, of course, you're not or you wouldn't be here. Do come on in! You must be freezing!'

She took me into the hall and helped me out of my coat beside the log fire as if I were an invalid and an elderly invalid at that. But despite that jarring squeaky voice which she couldn't help, she was being very pleasant and the fire was gloriously warm. I should have felt less frozen with nervousness. I didn't. I said mechanically, 'What a lovely hall,' then had a look round and found I had said the right thing.

The hall was oak panelled, long and narrow with a lowish ceiling and massive highly polished oak floorboards. The floor sloped slightly downwards towards the hearth that was large enough to take half an oak tree. The walls were hung with polished pewter trays and plates that caught the firelight. The main staircase ran up from the back of the hall to the first-floor landing. More solid oak. More polish.

June was pleased with my admiration. 'Endel's such a beautiful house and I do try to keep it nice. But it's quite impossible to keep all the rooms as I'd like as we've so many and you can imagine the staff problem! Do you know, when your father was a boy, your grandmother had nine resident maids and two men! And all I've got are my three dailies and old Murdo! You saw Murdo? He took up your things. We've given you your father's old room. We always called it Uncle Rosser's room. We thought you'd like that. Do you remember him?'

'I'm afraid not. He died when I was one.'

'As long ago as that!' That squeak nearly cracked my eardrums. 'Men and their silly pride! But dear old Grandfather was too old to change his ways so it's useless now to wonder why he didn't, but when we think of the way he treated his only granddaughter we get simply furious! Rose.' She put a hand on my shoulder. 'This last year you must have felt so terribly alone. We are determined you shall never feel like that again. You're Robert's first cousin and only blood-relative. Endel is your family home as well as ours and we want you always to remember that. Will you?'

I said, 'This is very kind of you –'

'Nonsense! Families should stick together and not have stupid quarrels. Tell me, dear Rose, do you still miss poor Charles dreadfully?'

I said, 'He was my husband.'

'And you can't bear to talk about him yet. Dear Rose.' She kissed me. 'I understand perfectly.'

She didn't, of course, but it was nice of her to make the attempt. It was nice of her to give me such a warm welcome. I was grateful even if I wished she would stop squeaking and touching me. I wondered how Robert stood both, and had a good look at her.

Her features were small and regular, but as she was so chubby they were rather lost in the expanse of her face. Her skin was poor for an Englishwoman of her age, which I put in the late twenties or early thirties. Her oatmeal twin-set and tweed skirt were of good quality, but being over a decade out of fashion for country wear, she looked dowdy. I noticed she was eyeing the height of my skirt hem, crochet stockings and high boots, and suspected she would have preferred me in black, but could have misjudged her as her expression gave so little away.

I apologized for causing Robert an unnecessary journey. 'I did try to ring from the station.'

'We guessed you had. It's too maddening all three lines should be down this afternoon.'

'All three?'

'Well, really it's just one line with extensions to the farm and End Cottage. David – he's our tenant at End – knew you were expected today and when he found his line was down he very sweetly came up to warn us in case we hadn't discovered the other two were broken. I know he's just longing to meet you, so I've asked him to stay to tea. Don't worry – he won't stay long!' She was the only person I had ever met who managed to squeak in a whisper. 'But I'm too fascinated to let him go without finding out whether it really was you he met in Austria. He vows it was, but doesn't expect you to remember him as you weren't introduced. He's in here.' She opened a door. 'Here she is at last, David! This is my sitting-room, Rose.'

Her sitting-room was small and newly decorated in crimson and white with the impersonal elegance of an ambitious but second-rate decorator. It had probably cost a bomb, but that hadn't succeeded in making it look like a room in a house in which people actually lived, wore muddy shoes or dropped cigarette ash. But all that I noticed later, when I got my mental breath back.

A man stood with his back to the log fire. A tallish, thick-set man in a grey roll-neck sweater and brown corduroys. His hair was thick and so fair that in the not very bright electric light it looked near-white. Charles' hair had been a much darker gold, but he had Charles' square-shaped face. His jaw was more pronounced, his mouth was wider and fuller, and Charles had only worn glasses for work. The two men could not have been twins. They might have been brothers.

His name was David Lofthouse and he had rented the cottage by the iron gates for six months. No one explained why and I didn't ask. June asked, 'Well, was it really Rose?' and then announced brightly that it really was a small world, wasn't it, and why didn't we all sit down and have a nice cup of tea as there was nothing like a nice cup of tea. As she handed me my cup, the lights flickered. 'Oh, no! Don't say that wretched Monster's going to break down with Robert out!' She jumped up. 'I'll just rush and get Murdo to look at it before he takes the dailies back home to Astead.'

'Murdo left five minutes ago with your helps. I saw them drive off.' The lights flickered again. 'If you don't switch on your emergency plant, June, we'll finish our tea in Stygian gloom,' said David Lofthouse. 'I'd offer to do it for you were I not too young and pretty to die.'

'Oh my word, David! What will Rose think!' June hovered, dithering. 'The Monster's just our name for the electricity plant, Rose. It's in the cellar under the hall and the emergency plant that runs off batteries is down under the kitchen. I don't much like switching over to the emergency when Robert and Murdo are out as I'm not good with machinery, and anyway the batteries last such a short time. Then we're down to candles! Oh, bother!' The lights were nearly out. 'I'll have to deal with it. It'll only take two ticks. You will forgive me?'

I smiled politely, 'Of course.'

David Lofthouse opened the door for her, then returned and offered me a plate of scones. 'Much less indigestible than the fatted calf.' He took one himself and sat down. 'How's the lad who twisted his knee, shaping?'

I made myself study him before answering. The shape of his head was different and so was his voice. The tone was much deeper and instead of Charles' Oxbridge he had a faint but unmistakable north-country accent. Perhaps not brothers, yet sufficiently similar to make me feel as if I'd been kicked in the stomach.

I said Adrian had done well and was due out of hospital and home tomorrow.

'Tough luck, his being kept in so long. How did you enjoy the rest of your holiday?'

'Very much, thanks.'

'No more icicles tried to clout you?'

I stiffened involuntarily. 'Not even one.'

'Good.' He raised his cup to me. 'You too are too young and pretty to die. Or didn't you realize the one I saw swooping past my camera lens could've killed you?'

'Yes,' I said, 'I did.'

He looked at me over the top of his black-rimmed glasses. The expression in his eyes was wary and shrewd. He didn't say any more and was still watching me in that way when June rushed back, panting. 'The joys of country life! I'll have to warn you, Rose, here in Endel that wretched Monster rules our lives! Now do have another cup of tea!'

CHAPTER THREE

The battery light was no stronger than candlelight. The light outside had nearly gone and the sky was a dark pewter. I glanced at David Lofthouse and wished I hadn't as the poor light had darkened his hair.

32

June was still running on about the electricity plant. 'Though it infuriates me, I dread to think what Endel must have been like without it. It works the electric pump as well as giving us light and heat upstairs. Can you imagine having to pump by hand every drop of water needed for a house this size? In the days when it was full of children and servants! But the trouble Robert had to persuade Grandfather to let him build it! The old can be so stubborn!'

I asked, 'Robert built it? Himself?'

'Most of it. The original installation just worked the pump. Robert's added to it so that we now have lights in the cellars, ground floor and first floor, and electric fires in all the habitable bedrooms, his study and my sewing-room. Robert's so clever!' June beamed with pride. 'David says Robert's Monster is an electric work of art!'

'And one that'd have any factory inspector foaming at the mouth,' said David. 'Touch the wrong switch and you'll light up like a Roman Candle.'

'David! You must stop trying to frighten Rose!' protested June. 'You mustn't let him worry you, Rose. You won't ever be expected to touch the Monster. Murdo looks after it very well on the whole, though he doesn't enjoy playing around with it as much as Robert.'

David said impassively, 'Possibly Murdo doesn't enjoy living dangerously to the same extent as Robert.'

June laughed as if he had made the joke that was going to keep her happy all week. 'Robert knows what he's doing."

'I'm sure he does, love.' He offered cigarettes, and when June and I refused lit one himself. We fell silent and the silence was uneasy. I didn't know why, or even if the unease was merely coming from myself. I just sensed it in the atmosphere and as June's guest felt I should try and break it. I asked David if he understood the machine.

'Roughly.'

'Roughly!' exclaimed June. 'For a physicist with a Ph.D., that must be the understatement of the year!'

'No.' He shook his head. 'Though I've a rough idea how it works, as I've frequently told Robert I find the fact it works at all a bloody miracle. And as I lack the Endel passion for living on a razor's edge, you'll have to hold a gun on me to get me to touch it.'

'Living on a razor's edge?' June's squeak sharpened. 'What do you mean?'

'Love, if that doesn't apply to a family that's chosen to live for centuries on land fifteen feet below sea-level with the sea less than a mile off, I don't know what does. Maybe to build a house on the side of a volcano might be more of a risk, though I'd not bet on it.'

'Is that all!' June dismissed the sea with a flick of her hand. 'Endel's strong enough to take on the sea.' She then told me about Midstreet village. I did not spoil her story by saying I had already heard it, but was a little surprised she did not throw in the legend of the Endels never dying in Endel. Then I remembered I was a born Endel and she was probably just being tactful. I remembered my parentage, but still without being able to accept the automatic follow-on. I was sitting in my old family home, but I could have been sitting in a hotel room. I would have liked to feel – here I belong. I was too on edge to feel anything but on edge. I sat thinking this over while the two others talked of tides, oil lamps and an occasion last November when End Cottage had been cut off for a week by the extra high tides flooding the main sea-dykes.

'You're certain it didn't bother you, David?' asked June. 'We were so worried about you.'

'Didn't bother me at all. If I'd not wanted isolation, I'd not have taken the place. Robert was very fair. He warned me about the tides, damp, loneliness and even the bloody ghost before he let me sign the lease.'

I roused myself. 'Your cottage is haunted?'

June looked worried. David was unmoved. He said, 'By reputation. After four months on and off in residence, I've yet to see or hear any sign of the supernatural. Possibly,

34

I'm too insensitive. Do you believe in ghosts?'

I said, 'I've an open mind.'

June laid a hand on my arm. 'You mustn't let this disturb you, Rose! Personally, I'm convinced End isn't haunted! Every tenant at End since I've been here has said just the same as David. I've never even heard of anyone who actually saw the ghost. Robert considers the idea pure rubbish, but as the marsh people are dreadful gossips and love passing on old wives' tales, he always warns new tenants so they won't think he was holding out on them when they hear the old tale.'

'Reasonable. And is Endel haunted?'

'Most certainly not!' She appealed to David. 'Tell her that's true!'

'True as they come, far as I know. Makes sense, too.'

'Why?' I demanded, guessing what was coming. June must have done the same as she was trying to catch his eye to get him to belt up. She did not succeed.

'Endel's scarcely had a chance to acquire ghosts has it? As you Endels, in general make a point of not dying under this roof. Of course your respected Grandfather beat the book on that, but as they tell us, there's to be an exception to prove every rule.'

June had flushed. 'David, that's just another stupid old wives' tale. I don't suppose Rose has ever heard it. Have you, Rose?'

'Vaguely.'

'Oh.' She pressed her lips together then smiled with an obvious effort. 'Then, in case it's disturbed you the way Robert says it did him as a kid, do let me remind you that not only Grandfather, but Robert's mother, died in Endel – and if the truth were known probably dozens of your ancestors.'

'You remember that,' put in David with a small sardonic smile, 'when the night closes in on Endel and the rafters moan and groan and the creepy-crawlies play tag in the beams and every warped board creaks like ghostly footsteps.' He walked to the window. 'Remember the night I spent here two months ago, June? I slept like a log, but before I dropped off I listened to Endel at night, and dead spooky it was.'

'Never bothered me,' June was getting worked up about the lights again. 'I wish Robert'd get back. The batteries are going to run out.'

'He'll be back in a couple of minutes. I thought I heard his car. See —' He stood away from the window. 'Turning off the sea-road now.'

She jumped up. 'Oh, good! And how I wish I'd your hearing, David! It's uncanny.'

'Born to be a gun-dog.' Again he opened the door for her. 'You catch Robert now, before he comes in, with luck he'll have enough battery light for working on the Monster.'

'Yes.' But she hesitated. 'I feel awful, leaving you again like this, Rose. Wouldn't you like to come and see Robert mend the plant?'

'As if any man in his right mind wants a couple of women breathing down his neck while he's on a job. And what woman in her right mind wants to be dragged from a warm fire to a freezing cellar? The lady'll be safe with me, love,' David insisted, before I could get a word in. 'We still haven't had a chance to compare more than the briefest notes on Austria. As nothing's so boring as listening while other people exchange mutual holiday reminiscences, we'll get them over while you're helping Robert. Unless' – he smiled at me – 'the prospect displeases you?'

Being a moral coward, I said, 'Oh, no.'

June said, 'I'll be quick as poss! I know Robert's just dying to meet you!'

He closed the door after her. 'This is going to be a very touching meeting.'

I said nothing.

He took June's seat on the sofa beside me. I had consciously to resist the urge to move away.

He said, 'Sometime I must show you the pictures I took

36

from that balcony. Or aren't you interested in photography?'

'I'm afraid not. Sorry.'

'Too bad. I got some good shots of the Alterberg. Good skiing, that mountain.'

'Yes. You'd skied it before?'

'No. I heard in Liederau it would be worth a trip up. I kept putting it off, then it was my last day, so I took it.'

'Quite a coincidence, my being there.'

'Wasn't it?'

'Particularly as you now live here.'

'That's right.'

'Of course you didn't know I'd be there.'

He said, 'I didn't know I'd run into an Endel at the foot of the Alterberg but directly I spotted you I knew you must be some relation. I asked around, heard your married name and where you were staying and came on up to chat of this and that with you.' He grinned. 'But the lady was not playing. Right?'

'Yes.'

He looked me over and laughed. 'Out of luck, aren't you?'

I let that ride. I had to, as I had no answer.

'What are you doing down here? Aren't you from the north?'

'Yorkshire.'

'Whereabouts in Yorkshire?'

'Near Wakefield. And do I miss all my industrial grime?' He switched into broad Yorkshire. 'Oh aye. I do that, lass.'

Charles had been a Londoner. It wasn't much of a relief. It was better than nothing. 'Why come to the marsh?'

'I like new places.' He went back to his normal voice. 'I was ill last year. My firm've obligingly given me six months off on full pay. The doctors told me to find a quiet spot by the sea. I saw an advertisement in a Sunday paper. I drove down to have a look and did a deal with your cousin Robert.'

37

'I see. What's your firm?'

'British Chemicals Consolidated. I've been working in their Coventry branch for the last five years. I've a flat there with four rooms and a dishwasher. I've let it to a man called Dick Evans and his wife. They're expecting their first kid this month. I run a Cortina, it's white and I've had it four months. I've no debts, no wife, no current mistress, or as far as I know, kids. For choice, I only drink Scotch and I smoke enough to get myself into an early grave. I've all the obvious vices and one or two I keep for special occasions. Anything else you want to know? Or will that do for a start?'

I flushed. 'I'm sorry. I didn't mean to be rude.'

He said, 'And who is that supposed to kid? Since you've had your go, I'll have mine. What're you doing here?'

'Isn't that obvious? Particularly as you were present when I discussed this project.'

He laughed again. He had good teeth. 'If you expect that to make me curl up with shame, I'd better tell you I'm singularly devoid of gentlemanly instincts. I didn't go to a public school, so you'll have to excuse a lad up from the working classes.'

'You're going to tell me you got a Ph.D. at night school after you left your Secondary Mod?'

'You've heard such establishments exist? You must read the *Observer*!'

'I do. I also recognize an ex-grammar chip when I see one. Good Grammar School? And, probably, Cambridge?'

'Bright girl. Yes to both.'

'Not particularly bright. I went to two Grammars myself and the last was co-ed. The girls didn't have chips. Most of the boys did, but as they were only sixth-formers I used to hope they'd outgrow them. Why don't you?'

He was very amused. 'Not only educated but also you can hit back. You're quite a girl.'

'Thanks,' I said dryly, 'though I still dislike eavesdroppers. Surely, you guessed we thought you a German?'

'Is it my fault I did German "A" Level and got my ski clobber in Munich?'

'You could have given us some hint!'

'And stop your chat? Don't be daft! I was fascinated.' I swallowed. 'At least, you're honest.'

'I am, when it suits me. So you decided to come, and now you've come, how do you feel?'

'I've not yet been here long enough to feel anything,' I lied.

'Like to bet?'

I was silent.

He said slowly, 'Doesn't the memory of your father's walking out of here bother you?'

'Not really. Why should it? All three men involved in that old row are now dead. It happened before I was born and when Robert was a baby. Why should either of us keep brandishing a hatchet we didn't raise in the first place – and don't even know why it was raised?'

'A point.' He looked thoughtfully round the room. 'You've not seen much of Endel yet. You've seen enough to appreciate this is some house.'

'Yes. And—?'

'And yet a man born and raised here turned his back on the lot. Must have been the hell of a bloody row to make him do that.'

'Obviously. Though as he was only twenty-one black may have looked blacker than black.'

'Your Grandfather wasn't twenty-one. He let it ride.'

'Maybe he didn't like his second son. Some fathers dislike their sons.'

'Now who's being obvious? The old boy must've hated your old man's guts.'

I winced before I could stop it. 'Was that necessary?'

'As I don't much care for euphemisms, yes. You don't disagree?'

'No.'

39

'But you'll lose no sleep over it?'

'As Robert's prepared to ignore the past, why shouldn't I do the same?'

'Why shouldn't you indeed.' He lit yet another cigarette. 'Though your immediate reaction was to turn down Robert's offer. Or have you forgotten?'

'No.'

'You're just glad you took your boy-friend's advice?'

'Since it was good advice, why not?'

'Good question. Here's another. Wasn't he a bit young for you? Or is he an Oedipal type? If so, aren't you a bit young for him? Where'd you pick him up?'

According to my mother I had inherited my father's quick temper. With Charles, I had learnt to control it. I didn't bother to do that now. 'I didn't pick him up! We met at Calais on the way out – and what business that is of yours, I'm damned if I know!'

'Don't be so dead grotty, love,' he said mildly. 'You know perfectly well why I'm making this my business. You knew as soon as I walked on to that terrace that I was interested in you. And you know it now.'

'I'm supposed to take that as a compliment?'

'Take it any bloody way you choose.' The lights were suddenly brighter and somewhere in the background there was a faint, regular thudding. 'Robert's got the job in hand. Any moment now and he'll be greeting you with glad cries. I know what he'll make of you. I wonder what you'll make of him?'

'I'll answer that when I've met him.'

'No ideas in your head until then?'

'As I said in another context, I try and keep an open mind.'

He stood up and looked at my legs. 'If you really want to perfect your *noli me tangere* routine you shouldn't wear a mini-skirt or that red sweater. Giveaway, that colour. Or didn't you know red's sexy?'

'I just happen to like the colour.'

'Even more of a giveaway. There may be hope for you, yet.'

I had my temper in hand. 'Thanks. That's made my day. But, tell me, Dr Lofthouse, aren't you in the wrong trade? Or do you do your stuff with a tape-recorder and a couch as a sideline?'

'Not me. I read pornographic literature to compensate for my lack of sex-life on the marsh. How do you cope with the problem? You must occasionally fancy a roll in the hay.'

'Unfortunately hay gives me hay-fever.'

'You poor kid! You should see a doctor – of medicine. For Christ's sake don't "Doctor" me here. If one uses that handle in a strange district, one invariably gets hauled out of bed in the middle of the night to deliver a baby. And for that aspect of reproduction, my dear Mrs D., I am not qualified. You'd better call me David and I shall call you Rose, though I must say it doesn't suit you. Too saccharine.'

'It happens to be a family name.'

He said thoughtfully, 'So your old man turned his back on all things Endel and then gave his only child a family name. If you'll forgive me saying so, you had a crazy mixed-up old man.'

'Possibly.'

'And Old Robert begat Richard and Rosser and Richard begat Robert and Rosser begat Rose. Stuck in the groove, you Endels. Have you always all had Christian names beginning with R?'

'I believe so.'

He said, 'Not only the same names over and over again, but the same faces, as you'll see when you take a walk along the first landing. You'll see your own dark hair and eyes and your own pale skin in every other old portrait hanging there.' He studied my face. 'Robert has your colouring, but you're much more like the rows of the dear departed than he is.'

41

'Probably as girls generally look more like their fathers and boys their mothers.'

'Precisely. And your father walked out and his daughter has walked back in. How do you explain that one?'

'Mid twentieth century.'

'With England swinging like we all know what and you all set to enjoy a jolly long weekend as a proxy returned prodigal. And the best of British luck! But as even the best can run out, mind if I offer you some advice? There'll be no charge.'

'If you want to.' He was silent. 'Well?'

'Just watch your step in Endel, Mrs D., just watch how you tread. There are a hell of a lot of odd wires trailing about this house and one or two could be live. I'm not saying they are. They just could be.'

I glanced at him curiously. He was probably acting, but he gave the impression of being suddenly very serious. 'If you honestly believe that, shouldn't you warn Robert rather than me? I don't understand anything about electricity. Strictly arts.'

He said, 'Your cousin Robert has the gifted amateur's true contempt for professionals and an admirable ability for looking after his own. But if you really don't recognize a live wire when you see one, you'd better take my advice, unless you want to end up as dead as you'd have been had that icicle landed on target.'

'You're making my flesh creep!'

'I'm not joking, woman!' He snapped. 'You might remember that!'

June practically exploded into the room, to my great relief. I neither liked nor trusted him, and his sudden change of mood had disturbed me more than I cared to admit to myself. I remembered my reaction to that chat with Herr Schneller. I could not forget that icicle and found it cold comfort that apparently he could not forget it, either.

June was gushing apologetically. I caught the last bit '... think me a terrible hostess! Robert's absolutely furious

42

with Murdo! He must have set the wretched thing wrongly this afternoon. Robert says it packed up because it was utterly overloaded. But here he is at last! Rose – this is your cousin Robert!'

CHAPTER FOUR

My mother had been born in 1917, but having been raised by her grandparents, her fundamental beliefs had been Victorian. Breeding, she said, mattered. Breeding, told. Had she met David Lofthouse socially she would have been as uncomfortable as she had been when I occasionally brought a schoolfriend home. She had been grateful for my State education, but saddened by what she had called 'the mixed influences'. At their only meeting she had been so pleased with Charles' patently upper-class manners, and bearing. She would have been as pleased with Robert Endel.

He was a slight man and he wore rough tweeds with elegance. We had the same colouring and if he was not the best-looking man I had ever seen, he was in the top five. He kissed me. 'Thanks for coming, Rose.'

I kissed him back. I found that surprisingly pleasant.

David removed himself. Robert had asked him to stay for our celebration drink, but much to my relief did not twist his arm.

After he had gone, Robert said he hoped I didn't think him too inhospitable to David, but this was a family occasion, and anyway David never liked staying long anywhere. 'Too restless, poor bloke.'

June had produced a decanter and glasses. Robert told her to put the decanter away as this was a time for champagne. 'I got up a bottle from the cellar just now. It's in the pantry.'

The pantry was the other side of the swing door at the far end of the hall that led into the kitchen quarters. June fetched the bottle at the double, then stood round making admiring noises while Robert pushed off the cork with his thumbs. He did it neatly, but as he was a fit man in the late twenties, despite his slight build I saw nothing surprising in his having strong wrists and fingers. But I wasn't his wife. Possibly he enjoyed a constant Greek chorus of admiration. He certainly got it from June. She reminded me of a television newsreel I had seen at the time Dr Nkrumah was running Ghana. 'Nkrumah can do no wrong!' the crowd kept chanting. June would have felt at home in that crowd if she could have substituted Robert for Nkrumah.

It was very good champagne, so after a second glass I asked if there was any special reason for their tenant's being so restless.

My cousins exchanged glances. Robert nodded briefly and June did the talking. 'We don't really know very much about David. We do know he's had a rather tragic background. He was involved in an accident at his work last year. Did he tell you?'

'Only that he'd been ill and given six months off. What happened?'

'Something he was working on blew up, killing two of his assistants and nearly killing him.'

Robert said, 'The poor bloke took the hell of an overdose of radio-activity.'

'He's a nuclear physicist? He didn't tell me.'

'He wouldn't,' replied Robert. 'It's not something he cares to discuss and probably he's not allowed to. He must have signed the Official Secrets Act or whatever it is people who work on those kind of jobs have to sign. He hates being reminded of the accident – and who blames the poor bloke? He was in charge at the time and one of the two killed was his mistress.' He looked at June. 'Weren't they hoping to get married last July when her divorce was through?'

'That's what he said that night he got very drunk and poured out the whole story. The night we put him to bed here.' She smiled at me. 'When he told you Endel at night sounded dead spooky I didn't like to remind him how much whisky he had taken before going to bed.'

'He often hit the bottle?' I asked.

They exchanged another glance. Robert said not unkindly, 'The poor bloke's got to do something down at End on his own. I wouldn't call him an alcoholic. Would you, June?'

She had to think about it. 'Not really. I will say this for him; he's very good about keeping out of our way when in one of his black moods.'

'He has moods?'

'God!' Robert smiled. He had an attractive and very gentle smile. 'One day he makes with a big hallo and the next ignores one's existence. Murdo, who sees more of him than anyone else as he keeps him supplied with logs and oil from my stores, says he's got an ugly temper, but I can't say I've ever seen it. As far as I'm concerned, he's an excellent tenant. That, believe you me, Rose, is a rare creature as any landlord'll tell you. I've had tenants at End who've assumed their lease included the run of this house, our garden and my farmland. The couple we had last spring and summer when Grandfather was ill were such a damned nuisance with their uncontrollable infant and dog that I had to shift my own sheep off my own land to safeguard the flock. After they cleared out I swore I'd never let the place again, as it's too near this house. Then David turned up last September having seen the advertisement my moronic solicitors had inserted without checking with me first. They'd been used to dealing with that side of things for Grandfather in the last few years and just went on as before after his death. They won't make a mistake of that nature again.'

'I should think not!' cried June.

I said, 'So David Lofthouse just turned up.'

'He did,' agreed Robert, 'and though I wasn't over-keen, as single tenants are generally the best bets from a landlord's angle, after some talk I let him have it. I've never had cause to regret it. He paid his full rent in advance, settles monthly with Murdo for fuel and oil for his lamps, stops by for tea with June about once a month and occasionally comes up for an evening drink. Otherwise he keeps out of our hair and we keep out of his.'

I said, 'He certainly sounds an ideal tenant.'

June was watching me. 'You don't like him?'

'He's not exactly my type. Probably very nice.'

They smiled. 'Oh well,' said Robert, 'these neurotic egg-heads aren't everyone's cup of tea. I hear you ran into him in Austria? Small world, indeed! But you won't have to see much, if anything, of him here.'

June squeaked, 'David won't like that! I think he's rather gone on Rose!'

'Which shows the poor bloke at least has excellent taste.' Robert drained his glass and set it down. 'If you girls'll excuse me, I'll now go and give that sod Murdo hell for overloading my machine.'

'I suppose it was Murdo?'

June had spoken. She grinned foolishly as we both stared at her. 'I'm not tight, honestly,' she giggled. 'I mean it! Was it Murdo? He doesn't usually mess up the Monster – not even on Saturday nights after calling at every pub on the marsh!'

Robert straightened his shoulders, tilted his head slightly to the left and raised one eyebrow. His stance struck a chord. It was not until later that I placed it. I stood in that way myself when suddenly startled.

'Darling,' he said, 'if three glasses of champagne has you suggesting that one of my tenants has tried to wreck my property, then you're on the wagon from now on. David may be a nut, but he's nobody's fool. He wouldn't bugger up my machine for no reason!'

'He had a reason! He wanted to get Rose to himself! He was determined to do that! Wasn't he, Rose?' I just shrugged. 'He could easily have got down into the cellars

46

during the afternoon. Anyone could. You know we never lock any doors.'

'Without the helps or Dolly seeing him? I doubt it, darling.'

The wine was beginning to hit me, if not as hard as June. 'Who's Dolly?'

'Grandfather's old labrador. She spends most of her time in the yard and anyone getting to the cellars'd have to pass her,' explained Robert. 'Did she bark, June?'

'She wouldn't.' June was getting peevish. 'You know that silly old bitch adores David!'

'How about the geese?' he demanded.

'Darling, they're always squarking!'

'Not without good reason, though I'll admit they're better watch-dogs than any dog.'

'Are they?' I asked.

'God, yes,' he replied. 'A dog may not bark at a friend, but geese shout at friend and foe alike. I keep six in a lean-to on the far side of the stables mainly to keep down the grass in the field beyond and also as I think them attractive birds to have about. They repay me by eating my grass and providing an infallible alarm system. They've grown accustomed to the normal comings and goings of the helps and ourselves, but let anyone, including ourselves, approach this house at what they consider the wrong time by day or night and they shout their heads off. With them around, we don't need a door bell. But you, my sweet June, need some black coffee. Murdo must wait while I get you some.'

'Robert's so thoughtful,' said June, 'he thinks of everything.' She flopped back in her armchair and closed her eyes. 'Aren't I lucky to have such a wonderful husband, Rose?'

I said, 'Yes.' It was probably the most truthful remark I had made since my arrival.

Robert produced the coffee then showed me my room.

'Your father's, for the first twenty-one years of his life. We thought you'd like that and do hope that in consequence you won't object to being on your own up this end of the house. Our room's along the other side. If you want anything, do shout, but good and loud. If you're nervous of the dark, please say and we'll leave the landing lights on all night.'

'How'll your Monster like that?'

'Not overmuch. It can take it –' he smiled. 'I hope.'

'There's no need on my account. I truly don't mind the dark.'

'Good.' He took one of my hands lightly in both his. 'Rose, I've not said this yet and I must. I'm so very sorry about your husband. Still hurt like hell?'

For once I didn't have to lie, or hedge. 'Yes.'

'Inevitable.' His fine-drawn face was sad and his rather thin lips curved sympathetically. 'You're so hellish young. Pity.' He then made me like him even more than I did from sight by not saying one day I would feel different. One day I would. One day I might be old; one day I'd certainly be dead, but neither future probability made a present analgaesic.

He talked about our fathers and Grandfather and repeated a lot of June's welcoming remarks but without sounding over-enthusiastic as she had. He said, 'I wish you'd stay longer than a long weekend.'

I explained needing a new job. 'I went to my last boss as a temporary last May, as he originally only expected to be in London a few weeks. He stayed until mid-December and had his wife fly over from the States to join him.'

'American, obviously?'

'Yes. He paid me so well I gave myself a winter holiday. Luckily, having a secretarial training, all one needs to get a job in London now is to pick up a phone. But I think I should go back on Tuesday or my agency'll start getting restive.'

'If that's what you want. We'll have another chat about

48

this, later. You must visit us again and often. I'd like that very much and so will June – particularly as she'll have to take things quietly for the next few months and Endel is more than somewhat off the map.'

I wasn't tight as June, but I was finding thinking an effort. I hoped that was just the champagne. 'June's not well?' Then I caught on. 'She's having a baby?'

He glanced down the long narrow corridor behind him before answering. 'We very much hope so, but as she's had a couple of misses, don't mention this to her unless she does. Our G.P.'s warned me she must take it very easily. So you'll not mind if we give you a rather quiet weekend?'

'Of course not! Congratulations.'

His eyes lit up. 'Thanks. As you'll understand, I want kids. This house needs 'em. And June's longing for a baby. She spends so much time alone here as I have to be up at the farm most of every day. She's very good and never complains, but I think the loneliness does get her down occasionally. She's not used to marsh life yet. Takes a lot of getting used to, unless you're born to it, or with it in your blood. I must say,' he went on thoughtfully, 'that's one thing about David that's always surprised me. I'd not have expected a city-dweller to have stuck it out so long, particularly in winter.'

'He said he liked the isolation.'

'He must. Still strikes me as odd. Yet, may not be. Perhaps after what he's been through he needs to hide out in the wilds and lick his wounds. Strange bloke, that.'

I said, 'Robert, I know what you said to June, but do you really think he wouldn't have fixed your machine today?'

'So you think he did, too?'

I said honestly, 'I don't know what I think.'

'Frankly, my dear,' he said, 'between ourselves, nor do I. But as no serious harm was done and I don't want June worried, officially I intend to blame Murdo and keep a rather closer eye than previously on my tenant. Don't you worry about him.' His smile was reassuringly grim. 'You leave him to me. I'll leave you now to unpack. See you at dinner.'

I smiled at the closed door. Suddenly, I felt safe and that was something I had not felt since the morning after my wedding day.

We had more wine at dinner, then spent hours over coffee, Robert and I swopping life histories, while June sat in a happy coma rousing herself only to refill our cups. Coffee normally kept me awake. I went out like a light directly I got into the high wooden-backed bed with boxed-in sides.

I woke abruptly a few hours later. It was very dark. I lay warm and lazy, wondering what had woken me and if I had the energy to reach out and switch on my bedside lamp to see my watch.

The wind had gone out with the tide. The sea made a sound of tearing silk against the beach beyond Midstreet Wall and somewhere an owl hooted. Then a fox barked and one of the geese squarked peevishly.

The old house muttered uneasily in sleep. The Monster two floors down thudded away with the regularity of a heart-beat and sounded louder in the quietness. Not the stillness. That was lacking. The roof-beams sighed, the floorboards creaked, an occasional door rattled on its hinges, a mouse scuttled in the rafters overhead.

Dead spooky, David had said. Dead right. Let my imagination have its head and those creaking boards could be footsteps.

Suddenly, I sat up. They were steps. They were too regular to be anything else.

And why shouldn't they be steps? Why shouldn't June or Robert be going downstairs for milk or a sandwich? Lots of people suffered from night starvation, and particularly pregnant women.

I listened more intently. If it were June or Robert, why

50

were the steps coming my way? Their room was up the other end.

I had not locked my door. I didn't intend locking it now. My reflexes worked so well I was out of bed and turning the key before my brain formed that intention. I was then ashamed of my folly and went back to bed, but I didn't unlock my door or lie down. I sat with the quilt over my shoulders, listening.

The corridor was long. The steps took quite a time to reach my door. It must be June being a good hostess and along to see if I was all right. 'June?' I called. Then, 'Robert?'

The creaks had stopped right outside my door. No one answered.

I knew the intelligent thing to do was to get up and see for myself. I was too much of a coward. I called again and more loudly. Again, no answer. I stayed sitting up and staring at the shadows round my door. As they were there, I couldn't have sworn the handle turned. I thought it did.

The creaks began again. Back along the corridor to the stairs. Back to my door. I counted four pauses at my door. After the fourth, when the creaks moved off they had a new sound. They came from the stairs. A few minutes, or it could have been hours, later, there was a soft click of a door closing somewhere below. No dog barked. But a chorus of geese cackled.

My reflexes were having a great time. I reached a window while the geese were still shouting. There was no moon, but my eyes had grown accustomed to the darkness and I could see fairly well. Nothing stirred below. I moved to the second window. It was circular, set high in the east wall and overlooked the end of the stables that stood across the yard behind the house. They had been built in a curve. The lower half now contained garages and Murdo lived in the self-contained flat above. I was just in time to see a man wearing what looked like a duffle-coat with the hood up, disappear into the shadow of the stables.

51

Presumably a ghost – if ghosts existed – might wear something that looked like a duffle, but open the door? Or disturb geese?

I went back to bed shivering with more than cold. If someone had been playing ghost to scare me, one thing was certain, he or she had done a great job.

I had no more sleep that night. When the first grey light crept in over the sea, and later the sun rose like a crimson paper lantern over the water, I was still unsure whether I had been the victim of a poor joke, my own imagination or something more sinister. Yet why that first, or last, I could no more explain than why that icicle, that machine's failure, or David Lofthouse's turning up in Austria on that specific day. All just coincidences? Possibly. And if not – what? Above all, why?

A dog began barking which roused the geese. 'Belt up, Dolly!' Robert shouted from a window, and the barking stopped. A little later there were steps in the yard, and then someone revved a car engine and drove off. I got up, unlocked my door and switched on the electric fire.

'Awake, Rose?' June came in with tea. 'You early bird! I hope this doesn't mean you slept badly?'

I assured her untruthfully I had had a splendid night just as I would have done any other hostess in similar circumstances.

'You English and your passion for fresh-air at night! No wonder you all get bronchitis!' She closed the window. 'It's so much colder this morning.'

I was surprised. 'Aren't you English?'

'On my mother's side. My father was Swedish. He died when I was nine and Mother brought me home to London. To her home, that was. She remarried the following year. My stepfather and I never hit it off, but as he's made Mother happy, I try to think on him kindly. For preference, I never think on him at all. They live abroad now.' She remained at the window. 'How did you get on with your stepfather?' she asked without turning.

'Well, thanks. He was sweet. Of course, I was older. Nine's not an easy age to take changes.'

'To be honest, no age would have been right for me, or my stepfather. He just wasn't interested in daughters and I expect I didn't like having to share my mother. It was a bit better after my brother was born.' Her eyes suddenly lit up with warmth. 'He was such a lovely baby. He was like a toy for me.'

'How lovely for you both. See much of him, now?'

'Don't I wish I did!' The light went out. 'My stepfather retired abroad – oh, look! There's another early bird!'

I joined her at the window. The early dew had frozen, the marsh sparkled with millions of frost diamonds and the dyke water glistened like brown glass. About a mile off, a man in a duffle-coat was walking towards the sea-road. The sunshine transformed his fair head to silver. I asked, 'Does your tenant often take early walks?'

'He's about at all hours of the day and night. He keeps his lamps burning so late I've often seen 'em when I've had to get up in the small hours. I really don't know when that man sleeps.' She waved to Robert below. 'He's off to the farm to start his men off. He'll be back for breakfast at eight-thirty. Suit you?'

'Fine, thanks.'

I stayed at the window after she left and saw David climb the steps over Midstreet Wall and disappear down the far side. I remembered June's remarking last night that no doors in Endel were ever locked. Presumably David Lofthouse knew that, too?

CHAPTER FIVE

Murdo was making up the hall fire. He had bushy eyebrows, large ears, a pointed chin and a voice that fell like soft water from his tobacco-stained lips. He came from

Glasgow and had arrived on the marsh with an old Scottish zoologist who had since died. Robert had taken him on last June, as gardener in the summer and odd-job man in winter. His main jobs seemed to be the fires and ferrying to and fro from Astead the three dailies. They worked from eight to four-thirty each weekday, until noon on Saturdays and all four members of the domestic staff had Sunday off. June said she loved Sundays. 'All day we have our beloved Endel to ourselves.'

One of the helps came through the swing door with a huge vase of mimosa as Murdo and I were exchanging good mornings. She had kicked the door open and a fat black labrador hurled itself under her foot and at my legs.

'Down, Dolly!' The woman scolded in an anxious whisper. 'You'll ruin the young lady's stockings, and you know Mrs Endel don't allow you this side the house! Murdo, fetch her out!'

Murdo grinned slyly. 'Och, the wee doggie's doing no harm! I see you've no aversion to making her acquaintance, ma'am.'

'Indeed, not. She's cute.' I patted the amiable creature now sitting on my feet and thumping her tail. 'Hi, Dolly!'

Murdo continued to grin, but the help was in a tiz. She was youngish and had a pleasant face. 'She's a dear old thing, but she can't stay in this hall. I'm sorry, madam, but Mrs Endel don't fancy dogs.' She held open the swing door. 'Come along, Dolly! Out you go!'

'Murdo!' June was on the stairs. 'Please take that animal away! Farm dogs belong on farms not in houses! Really, Mrs Franklin! You know my views!'

Dolly was stubborn. Murdo had to haul her off by the collar, clucking encouragingly, 'Will ye come away now, ye wicked wee doggie!'

Mrs Franklin hurried off with her mimosa. 'The staff are too bad, Rose!' June's squeak was still outraged. 'As if I can help being allergic to dogs! If this hall wasn't so large, already I'd be sneezing my head off.'

I made sympathetic noises and threw in my own allergy to hay. She said surely that was no problem as there were dozens of proved antidotes. I didn't explain that to date I hadn't discovered one that worked on me as she clearly was not interested. She was, I suspected, one of those people to whom any problem that didn't happen to be her personal problem, did not exist. She suddenly reminded me of a maths mistress at school who had done everything short of beating me over the head with the blackboard when she found me incapable of grasping the elements of algebra. In repose, she had had June's blank face and wide empty eyes, though she had been a brilliant mathematician as well as a poor teacher. She had also been a Queen Bitch, though new girls at first thought her 'so sweet'. I had not thought of her in years. She was in my mind over breakfast as I watched June go into another admiring orbit round Robert.

'Darling.' She sugared his tea, and buttered his toast. 'I know how devoted you are to old Dolly, but she's fourteen and life must be a burden for her now she can't get her exercise up at the farm. Is it really kind to keep her? She's so obese.'

'Labrador bitches can run to fat in old age,' grunted Robert into his newspaper. 'Dolly's happy enough to live her lazy life in the yard.'

I asked if I could take her for a walk or two over the weekend?

'You like walking, Rose? On mud!' June's voice hit a new high. 'You must be joking!'

'No. I love it. May I, Robert?'

'My dear girl.' He lowered the paper, smiling. 'You don't have to ask my permission. You can come and go and do anything you wish. If you want to walk Dolly, do so any time. She's wise as they come and'll keep you off the boggiest stretches of marsh and the bits of quicksand on the beach. I think you'll find the farm beyond her range, but if you do stroll up there, all I beg is that you shut any gate you open and keep off newly ploughed land as it may be newly sown.'

June said before I walked anywhere I must see all round Endel.

She started her tour directly after breakfast. We went straight upstairs as she had briefly whisked me through the kitchen quarters last night and Mrs Hodges, the cook, had the usual cook's antipathy to invaders in her kitchen. We began on the second floor. I lost count of the number of bedrooms with draped four-poster or brass Victorian bedsteads. They were all clean, but smelt of damp. 'Too many to heat,' said June, 'as the Monster doesn't yet reach this floor. Let's go down.'

I would have liked to take more slowly the rows of old family portraits on the first-floor landing and corridor walls. June wanted me to admire the new bathrooms. 'Ours. Along here' – she swept me past fading Endel faces with the men's dark hair curling to their shoulders – 'our official guest-room. Tell me, do you like the curtains?'

'A charming pink,' I lied.

'I think pastels are the only colours for bedrooms.' She opened another door. 'Robert's study.'

Outside the study were the Victorian Endels, the men with full beards and their ladies simpering primly. I stopped in the corridor. 'Is Grandfather here?'

She glanced at me oddly. 'His room?'

'No. His portrait?'

'Oh, that! It's in the drawing-room. My show-piece, so I'm keeping it till last. That door was his room.' She didn't open it. 'I must show you my sewing-room.'

This lay at the far end and next door to my room. It was fitted with an angled lamp, electric sewing-machine, cutting-out table and drawing-board for patterns. 'How very professional, June!'

'Sewing's my hobby. I make all my own clothes. I love making things.'

She was wearing another twin-set and skirt and this

morning, pearls. I congratulated her genuinely on her skill, if rather less than that on her fashion-sense. She even wore court shoes. The last pair I had seen had been on my mother roughly ten years ago. Her get-up intrigued me. Last night she explained living several years in London before meeting Robert at a party and marrying him shortly after, two years ago. I remembered how out of fashion my own clothes had seemed when I got back to London after my two years in Spain, and spent my first week in my present flat putting up hemlines. June's now was below her knees. Maybe Robert liked long skirts on his wife? From the glances he had given my legs, he did not object to minis on widowed cousins. Yet June had very good legs. If I had a husband as attractive as Robert and her skill with a needle, I'd get busy and fast on my hems. I couldn't conceive why she didn't and why she apparently never looked at a fashion magazine or newspaper article.

The next stop on our tour was the dining-room. It was a vast room. The table she informed me was sixteen feet long and five wide. It looked it. 'You and Robert'd need walkie-talkies if you ate often in here.'

'Plus a spare fortune to heat it. That's why we use the morning-room for all but formal occasions. Grandfather, of course, refused to eat anywhere else. This was his favourite chair.' She hovered behind, but did not touch, the stiff high-backed chair with claw arms at the head of the table. 'Sometimes I can almost see him still sitting here.' She shivered and not surprisingly as the room was icy. 'This is the only room in Endel I don't like. It's got a sort of funny atmosphere. Don't you notice it?'

'Only that it's a bit chilly.'

'It's more than that. I've often wondered,' she mused, 'if it's anything to do with that old row.'

'It took place in here?'

'Grandfather would never discuss it, but as he would thrash out family problems over meals and was such a creature of habit, I'm sure it did.' She touched my arm.

'You won't let this worry you?'

'Oh, no.' Yet if she seriously did not want to worry me, why hadn't she kept her theory to herself? Or had she spoken without thinking? Possibly. I thought of that maths mistress. Possibly not. I was Robert's cousin, not hers, and though she was still trying to keep up the big welcome, the strain must be telling. Also, the way in which Robert and I had clicked at sight couldn't have given her much cheer and with that I did sympathize. I had been a wife.

'Now, my beautiful drawing-room!'

Theoretically, she was right. It was a beautifully proportioned room and every piece of furniture was a well-chosen antique. The upholstery was ice-blue, the carpet was pale grey, the walls and curtains were white. It looked and felt cold as a tomb. The chill ran down my back as June closed the hall door behind us and I had to pack the false enthusiasm into my voice.

'You must see Robert's parents.' She opened a glass cabinet and handed me a twin photograph set in red velvet. Richard Endel wore Second World War Army uniform. Robert had inherited his father's hair, eyes and straight nose, but not his loose sensual mouth and weak chin. Hélène Endel's very pretty face made me catch my breath. 'She's only a kid here!'

'Nineteen. They met as students at the Sorbonne. Or did you know?'

'Only that she was French and died in childbirth.'

'Tragic.' She studied the faces with an affection she must have assumed for Robert's sake since she could not possibly feel it for two people she had never met. She replaced the photographs in the cabinet. 'Don't you think my father-in-law looked fascinating?'

'Very good-looking.'

'Aren't all you Endels?'

I smiled weakly.

She said, 'Charming and brilliant, was Grandfather's description of his eldest son. And in any crises, he went to pieces, as very brilliant people so often do. Like poor David,' she added in afterthought.

'He goes to pieces?'

'Well, dear, firms don't usually give obviously outwardly healthy employees six months off on full pay without good reason. They must hope the clean quiet country air'll heal whatever damage his experience has done to his mind. The war prevented Richard Endel from having time to slow down.'

'Slow down from what?'

She made sure the door was closed. 'The staff will gossip. Robert'd hate that. He hates any mention of the night he was born – just as David hates any mention of that work accident. Robert, at least, can't possibly be responsible for the event he likes to forget. He was in arms.'

'What happened?'

'I shouldn't really tell you,' she said, which showed she had every intention of telling me. 'But you know he met Hélène at the Sorbonne? Well, Grandfather had always intended him for the Diplomatic Corps. Richard got his First at Cambridge and was only meant to be in Paris one year. He was of age. He met Hélène and they married secretly. Grandfather was furious. He went over to Paris to read the riot act and luckily took one of his rare great likings to Hélène. He stayed in Paris some months, then brought them back here with him. Three weeks after they arrived Robert was born four weeks prematurely in this room.'

'Why in here? She died in here?'

'They were at dinner when she suddenly went into labour. She spoke very little English and only Richard spoke fluent French. He just crumpled. Grandfather took over, had the servants bring down a bed as he didn't dare move her even upstairs, and then rang every doctor on the marsh and in Astead. But it was November.'

She had paused expectantly. I asked, 'What's so special about November?'

'I forgot – you're new to the marsh. November and February are the two worst months for our mists. We may get one while you're here this weekend. There was one that night. It had started during the afternoon and directly it was dark, Endel was shrouded. It can be. It can be so bad that not even a marshman'll risk moving.'

'And that night?'

'Everything was against them. Their family doctor who was one of Grandfather's oldest friends, was ill himself with bronchitis. He had a young assistant locum who was very good – and had been called out to deliver another baby in Shepland. That's a village right across the marsh. He eventually reached Endel on foot in the small hours. By then, Robert was born. Grandfather saved his life. He knew nothing about human medicine, so treated the tiny baby as his shepherds treat premature lambs. He wrapped Robert in shawls, gave him drops of brandy and put him in a clothes-basket in the airing cupboard. The young doctor couldn't praise Grandfather enough for what he'd done for Robert, but unhappily there was nothing anyone could do for poor little Hélène. She had a bad haemorrhage and needed blood. The doctor tested everyone's in the house including his own, but none matched. He tried to get an ambulance out. One started from Astead, but couldn't get through the mist in time. The doctor was with her when she died.' She was silent. I didn't break it. I felt I should. I felt this was the last subject a pregnant woman should dwell on, even though she had brought it up. But the thought of that November night haunted me as I seemed to sense it still haunted that room. To me it was a nightmare room, and I could not get out of it fast enough.

June had not finished. 'Do you know what Richard Endel did all that night?'

I shook my head.

'Walked. Up and down that first-floor corridor. Along to his room – now my sewing-room – back to the stairs. Just up and down. Can you imagine that?'

My mouth had gone dry. I had nothing to say.

'Years after, when Grandfather eventually told me all this, he said he'd never been able to get the sound of his son's footsteps that night out of his head. Goodness knows he was the last man to indulge in foolish fancies! He dismissed that stupid Endel legend as damned rubbish! "We Endels are a violent breed," he'd say. "Violent men expect to die violent deaths like men, not cosseted in their beds like old women!" Poor darling.' She smiled tenderly. 'He was so cross when he knew he was dying peacefully. He got even crosser when people said End Cottage was haunted. He refused to believe in ghosts, yet I always believed he came close to thinking Endel was haunted by his eldest son. Of course, all that was part memory, part imagination. Don't you agree?' She shot a keen glance at me. 'You've gone white! I haven't upset you?'

'June, I'd have to be made of iron not to be upset. It's a sad story.'

'And you've had so much sadness in your life, already. I shouldn't have told you. I talk too much. Come and have a better look at Grandfather. It's such a wonderful portrait. It'll take your mind off the past.'

If my logic was bad, hers was worse. Had I not been so shaken I would have been amused. If anyone was responsible for the past that had made Robert and I what we were in the present, it was the man painted in the portrait that hung over the wide, cold hearth.

June said, 'This was done in 1938.'

Old Robert Endel had been painted in his favourite chair and wearing comfortable tweeds. The material was the only comfortable element in the painting.

'Well, Rose? What do you think of him?'

I chose my words. 'Remarkably handsome, even in middle age.' I studied the hard brown eyes, tight thin lips and formidable jaw. I left those bits out. 'Fine head of hair.'

'It was white when I knew him, but up to his first stroke

61

he was as upright as he looks there. And he had such magnetism. Originally' – she giggled archly – 'he frightened me, just a teeny bit! Then we made great friends – though he wasn't a man to show his feelings.'

I resisted the temptation to say the face in the portrait looked incapable of feeling for anyone but himself. I was no longer surprised my father had walked out. All that did surprise me was that it had taken him twenty-one years to do so.

'Excuse me, madam,' Mrs Franklin had come in. 'Mrs Wenden would like a word with you on the telephone.'

June made a moué. 'What does she want? Won't be a moment, Rose.'

Mrs Franklin lingered to admire the portrait. 'Fine-looking gentleman he was, seemly, madam.'

'Didn't you know my grandfather?'

'Oh, no,' she said. 'I only come here to work in September the week after Mrs Hodges started – no! I tell a lie! It was Mrs Smith as cleans upstairs who come the week afore me and Mrs Hodges the week after! But that Murdo'll recall the old gentleman! Murdo come in June just afore old Mr Endel had his stroke. Shame! But we all got to go when our time come and this won't get me sitting-room floor done!' She turned, then turned back. 'So you was a Miss Endel, madam?'

'Yes. My father was Mr Rosser Endel.'

'So Mrs Endel was saying. And you lost your husband? Shocking! A young lady like you. Young gentleman, was he?'

'Thirty-two.'

'Accident?'

'Plane.'

'Tck. Tck. Tck.' She clicked her tongue against her teeth. 'Never did trust them things. My hubby wanted me to fly over to France for our holidays last year. He couldn't get me up. And what's wrong with old England, I says, so we went down to an holiday camp instead. Had a lovely stay we did. Off there again this weekend, we are. My hubby's got the two days owing from work, so Mrs Endel says it'll be all right if I don't come in Saturday or Monday.' She had another look at the portrait. 'No offence, madam, but I can't see him giving me the extra time off. One of the old school he looks, and not one as I'd fancy crossing nor get nowhere if I did! Good thing young Mr Endel's different what with the match this Saturday and all!'

I doubted June would approve of my gossiping with the helps, but I loved a good gossip. 'What match is this?'

'Astead Town plays the Marsh Villages, Astead ground Saturday afternoon. There'll not be standing room in Astead this Saturday and if it's a draw Saturday night and there'll be murder done! Football! Don't ask me what it do to a man, but we lives near the ground and there's many a Saturday afternoon a body can't hear herself think! Ever so glad I am my hubby don't fancy the game, but you should hear that Murdo and the men up the farm! Come noon Saturday and like as not there'll not be a man left down the marsh!'

'I didn't realize marshmen were such ardent football fans. Wouldn't they have the half-day in any case?'

'Official like, yes, madam. But with this weather holding dry and the spring ploughing started, there's many a farmer as'd want his men to work the overtime and create cruel if they turned it down. There's not much work for a man off the land round here and the men knows it. Young Mr Endel'll know it too, but he said as he gives his word they'd have time off for the match and the time off they'll have!'

I was faintly shocked to find how pleased I was at this further evidence of Robert's amiable nature. 'Sounds like a jolly weekend all round.'

'Enjoy yourself while you can, is what I always says, madam! Only got one life – and this won't buy the baby no new frock!' She opened the door. 'Oh, it's you, sir!' she exclaimed to someone in the hall. 'Good morning! Wanting Mrs Endel? She's on the study phone, but the other young lady's in here.' She ushered in David Lofthouse.

He wore a duffle-coat over a city suit and was off to London for the night and probably, he said, all weekend. 'I let the Endels know when I'm going to be away in case they miss my smoke signals and start dragging dykes.' He looked at the portrait. 'Paying your respects to your late – if only lamented by Robert – grandad? And a right bloody-minded bastard he looks up there!'

I agreed though I had no intention of saying so to him even if his news had made my day. 'June appears to have been very attached to him.'

'For Robert's sake she'd try and love Old Nick himself. For Robert, she'd go through fire and drink water – as even you must have already rumbled.'

As I was unlikely to have to see him again in the next few days and would postpone my next visit until his tenancy ended, I ignored that 'even you'. 'She's a very devoted wife.'

'Plus, plus.' He looked at me over his glasses. 'Lucky man, Robert. Adoring wife, highly decorative cousin, beautiful home. Who says no one can win 'em all?'

I said, 'I expect he has his problems.'

'If not now, he'll have had 'em living with that old bastard up there. The Old Devil, as they still refer to him, locally. Your father, incidentally, whom a few local people still remember, is spoken of as a lively young gent with no vice in him. Favoured his mum, they say, and she were a real nice lady, Mr Lofthouse, sir.'

I was more interested than I cared to show. 'Do you really know this? Or are you making it up?'

'My sweet Mrs D.,' he drawled, 'sure, I know it. I know everything. I'm an idle layabout with nothing to do but walk and talk and hours to waste in local pubs. You name a marsh pub. I know it and they know me. And if you think simple country folk don't open up to strangers, you know

64

damn all about the simple country life. One "how do" and you can't get a word in for hours.'

I thought of Bert Mercer and Mrs Franklin. 'So I've gathered.'

'Have you, indeed?' He took off his glasses to polish them, and blinked myopically. 'And what do you think of old Iron Guts up there?'

'An interesting face. Endel colouring, but not a typical Endel. Too tough.'

He replaced his glasses to scan my face. 'He's not untypical. You Endels are tough cookies. Any family that's survived as long as yours has had to be tough, dead crafty, and dead good at keeping one eye permanently fixed on the main chance. That's how your lot hasn't gone to the wall.' He glanced up. 'I'd lay odds on, that at Robert's age he looked just as Robert does now.'

'Rubbish!' Indignation made me thoughtless. 'Robert's got such a kind face!'

'So he's being kind to you? Bully for Robert. Bully for you – though I wonder how June likes it?'

I flushed, 'Do you have to make cracks all the time?'

'I've a nasty suspicious mind, love. You'll have to love me for what I am and not for what I haven't got.'

'I'll bear that in mind.'

'You do that.' He yawned. 'Sorry. I was up most of last night. I kept meaning to go to bed. Too lazy to make the effort. You sleep well?'

'Very.' I eyed his duffle-coat. 'Thanks.'

He came closer. I had stepped back before I realized it. He said drily, 'I've my nasty habits, but they don't include rape – at least, not first thing in the morning after a rough night.'

There was nothing I could say so I said nothing.

'May I ask you something, Rose?'

'If you want to.'

'Is it my after-shave? Do I need advice from my best

friend? Or do I just look like him?'

His insight was more than disturbing. 'Whom?' I asked in pretence.

'You know who. The late Charles D.'

I looked at the floor. 'He was very fair. About your height.'

'Was he, indeed?' He paused. 'He beat you up?'

I looked up. 'Of course not!'

'Too bad. If he had, you might've learnt how to defend yourself.'

'You think I need that?'

'Who doesn't?'

We were fencing again. It wasn't only for the usual reason. I was quite certain of that without being able to explain why to myself. 'How do you manage? Judo?'

'Karate.' He grinned. 'You should see me with a block of wood.'

'What's this about wood?' June had come back. She was very full of the conversation she had just had with this Mrs Wenden who lived at Shepland and had known my father and his brother as boys. 'Her family come from St Martin's. She's a dear old thing, but the most fearful bore. She wanted us to lunch with her tomorrow. I explained we couldn't possibly leave Robert as everyone'll be away owing to the match. I hope you don't mind, Rose, but I hate leaving my poor Robert to fend for himself. I promised her you'd be down again soon and then we'd all meet. I couldn't think how she knew you were here until she said you'd told her, David.'

'Was that wrong, then?' he queried.

'Oh, no! It's just that for Rose's first visit we do rather want her to ourselves. But I didn't know you knew the Wendens. Where did you meet?'

'Hitching a lift out from Astead one day my car had packed up. I just hope the bloody thing doesn't pack up today.' He explained his trip to town. 'If I don't push off now, I'll be in trouble.'

June smiled coyly. 'Got a date?'

'What do you think?'

I watched them both and thought of June's story, those steps in the night, and looked at his duffle-coat. If he knew the whole story of Robert's birth night, which was highly probable, it could have been his idea of a joke. That should have been as much a relief as his leaving for London. Possibly it wasn't for the simple reason that Charles had had an odd sense of humour. And yet I locked my door again that night.

I was still awake when the irregular creaking altered to regular footsteps hours later. Five pauses outside my door, that night. My door? Or the sewing-room? I was too rattled to tell the difference.

When I woke in the morning, my pillow was damp with sweat. I remembered hearing no door click downstairs and no uproar from the geese, but I went into the corridor and looked out at End Cottage from a landing window. There was no smoke from the chimney and when I searched the marsh for a walking figure, the marsh was empty. At breakfast my cousins remarked on my pallor. 'Are you really sleeping well?' insisted June.

I made the excuse of having had one of my occasional bad dreams.

'Only to be expected,' said Robert kindly. 'When anyone goes through a bad patch, nature always takes out the change in bad dreams. Would you like to move into the guest-room? It's nearer ours.'

Being a moral coward I said that really wasn't necessary. June was satisfied. Robert continued to glance at me anxiously throughout the meal.

CHAPTER SIX

The helps were in holiday mood that Saturday morning. Murdo whistled tunelessly through his teeth as he heaved round his log basket, the upstairs cleaning lady hummed a pop tune as she did Mrs Franklin's work as well as her own. I wished I could share their mood. I made an effort and did try to sound as enthusiastic as June at the prospect of the special outing Robert had arranged for that evening. 'He's booked a table at the Woolpack in Shepland. Wonderful food! You'll love it, Rose! Shall we have our coffee now?' June hurried across the hall and slipped on the new polish, falling on her outstretched right hand. 'Oh, damn! I've put my wrist out again!'

Mrs Smith, the upstairs help, had rushed with me to assist June. 'Again, madam! I'm ever so sorry! You ought to get the doctor to see to that wrist proper! It'll not be right till you do!'

'I suppose I must.' June flexed her fingers. 'I do so loathe doctors! I'll go and put on my old wrist strap now. Oh, no!' She frowned impatiently. 'I've just realized this means Robert won't let me drive and I wanted to drive us both up to the farm this afternoon. I'm not walking all that way, but I know Robert's longing to show you round. Can you drive, Rose? Got a licence?'

'Yes.' It wasn't her wrist that was bothering me. She had not fallen hard, but she ought not to fall at all. 'June, do come and sit down. Can I get the coffee?'

She looked about to refuse, then changed her mind. 'Perhaps I should. Will you, Rose?' She did not mention her pregnancy until we were shut in the sitting-room with our coffee. 'I don't think it'll have hurt me. Do you?'

'Quite honestly, I don't know.' As she had now admitted to being three months on the way, I added, 'Robert said your doctor thinks you should take things very quietly. Why not lie down till lunch?'

'That might be wise.' She held my hand. 'You can guess what this means to us both. But what'll you do?'

'I'd rather like a walk. Can I take Dolly?'

'If that's your idea of pleasure, dear, with pleasure!'

I was glad to get out of the house. The feeling of oppression with which I had woken was getting me down. A walk might lift it.

Murdo was chatting to Dolly in the yard. She and I had not met since our short walk yesterday afternoon. She greeted me as if back from South America.

Murdo produced a lead. 'Not that ye'll be needing it, ma'am. She's aye an obedient wee doggie. Ye've a fine morning for a stroll.'

'I hope it keeps fine for your match.'

'Och, aye. It will that.' He surveyed the sky. 'There'll maybe be a wee gale this night. Yon clouds have the look of that to my way of thinking.'

There was something I wanted to ask him. This was the first chance I had had away from the house and other ears. Though Endel was so large and Robert was so often out at the farm, somehow June was always around. Since, despite her constant song and dance on the joy of having me in Endel, I had yet to feel she liked me, I guessed to shadow a guest was her idea of being a good hostess.

To pave the way now, I asked Murdo if a gale would upset the Monster.

'Och, no. We've no outside wires or cables.'

'Good. Then it won't pack up again.'

'Ye'll be thinking of ye'r first evening, ma'am?' The little man faced me, irately. 'It was the overloading that caused the breakdown then and I'd have ye ken I'd no part in it as I was telling Mr Endel! I'd not press the wrong switch! Am I not a fitter by trade?'

'You are? I'm sorry, Murdo. I didn't know.'

'Och, ye've no way of knowing.' He mellowed, slightly.

'I'm telling ye I'd fifteen years on the job in Glasgow before I was away to the war and took a bullet in my chest. I'd then to work in the open, and as I've aye had the green fingers, I took to gardening. But a fitter I was first.' He rolled every 'r' violently. 'A fitter would not make a mistake of that nature, I'm telling ye!'

'I'm sure you wouldn't. But – why did it break down? I mean, who pushed down the wrong switch?'

His crafty face closed exactly as if he had shut a door between us. 'I've no idea, ma'am.' He picked up an empty log basket and stomped off towards the cellar door.

I looked after him thoughtfully, then whistled to Dolly. 'Heel, chum.'

She ambled down the cinder road beside me sniffing new and old smells. She had no problems. She didn't care who was lying or why my first night's 'ghost' had had to leave the house and last night's been content to stay put.

We reached Endel's gates. I stopped to look at End Cottage. It was shut and silent and in the main dyke that divided it from the road two swans were raising a family of cygnets.

Suddenly, with her nose on the trail, Dolly scampered across the dyke bridge to the front door and began sniffing at the doorstep. 'Dolly, you mug, back! There's no one home.'

She might normally be obedient, but I had to call several times before she left off and recrossed the bridge so obviously reluctantly that I had another long look at the cottage. The windows looked back at me blankly and nothing stirred visibly inside. Dolly was staring at it fixedly.

'What can you scent?' I asked her. 'The ghost?' She wagged her tail. 'So you don't get scared like me?' I hesitated, then decided to experiment. 'Think there's someone in there? Find him, Dolly!'

She was off at once. She raced over the bridge and scratched on the front door. No one opened it, or appeared at a window. I waited another minute or so, then called her off, feeling even more thoughtful. Either old Dolly was another nut-case, or there was someone in End.

We climbed the steps up the Midstreet Wall, then sat on the top in sight of, but not facing the cottage. I watched it covertly. I saw no one and it could have been imagination, yet I had the distinct impression of being watched. A passing tramp, as David was still in London? Wouldn't Dolly have barked or growled in that event, instead of acting as if whoever was inside was an old mate?

It was pleasant up there on the wall. Almost too pleasant for disturbing problems. Only almost, so the problems niggled though I enjoyed the feel of the sweet, salty breeze in my hair and the sight of the sea a long way out and muttering gently. The tide was just on the turn. The wide stretch of sand beyond the pebbled beach looked very inviting. The gulls knew the stretches of quicksand as well as Dolly and were sitting in lines on the safe patches, chattering together. A long row of sea-birds lined the now exposed terracotta pipe that drained the main dyke under the wall and hundreds of yards off into the sea. The pipe was wide enough to take a man's body. Robert said occasionally that actually happened, but more often in spring and autumn when the tides were highest, an unwary sheep slipped into the water and was carried out. He had warned me as stringently as Bert Mercer about the dykes. 'They're deeper and more deadly than they look. Those rushes are ten feet tall or more and beneath them are feet of sludge. If you slip in, the reeds tangle your legs and the sludge sucks you down, so stay away from the edges. You've marsh blood, but you've not been here long enough to have the true feel of the marsh. The only people who come out of our dykes alive, are marshmen. And before you can call yourself a marshman, you've to fall in twice!'

'You've done that?' I asked.

He laughed. 'God! Dozens of times! It's a wonder I'm not web-footed!'

The thought of his laughing face made me smile. What-

71

ever I had or hadn't expected about Endel, I hadn't expected Robert or the immediate affection we had both formed for each other. I wasn't generally so certain about men. I was with Robert. I was so certain that I realized unless I was very careful and even more, sensible, I would find myself with a top problem to beat all others.

The sight of Murdo's leaving the house with the two helps made me get up. 'Home, Dolly. Lunch.'

Again Dolly wanted to call in at End Cottage. I looked at it hard and walked on by.

June was in the hall admiring her pewter. 'Mrs Smith gets it even brighter than Mrs Franklin. And she's not such a talker. I do so dislike cleaners who waste hours holding a duster and nattering.'

'Mrs Franklin seems a good worker. And how convenient their all living in Astead, though isn't that rather far for you to have to fetch them?'

'Murdo doesn't mind. Why should he, as Robert foots the bill? Anyway, Astead women are much better workers than marshwomen – if any would work here.'

Something in her tone made me ask, 'They won't?'

She smiled thinly. 'Marsh folk don't like working for outsiders, my dear, and though I'm mistress of this house, that's what I am to the marsh. Don't think I care!' From her expression, she cared a lot. 'I was a little hurt when all the women who worked here in Grandfather's time gave notice after his death, but now I've my nice Astead staff, I'm glad.' She pressed her face to the hall window. 'Good! Here comes Robert's car from the farm!'

Robert left us early after lunch as there was some field he wanted to finish ploughing before showing us round. I had hoped during lunch for some chance to tell him privately about Dolly's odd behaviour at End. I did not get it. We had a cold meal and June never left the table.

Robert looked into the morning-room as we cleared the dishes. 'Sure you can manage June's mini?'

'Quite. Charles had a mini.'

It was the first time I had volunteered that name. June looked as if I had made an improper remark – a not uncommon reaction, as any widow and probably widower, discovers. Robert was only mildly interested. 'What did you do with it?'

'It wasn't paid for. The garage took it back in lieu of the rest.'

His dark eyes softened. 'Finances tight as that?'

'Free-lance writers who don't hit the big-time usually live in the red. Either they learn to live with that, or go into another business. It's all right, so long as the output keeps up. If it suddenly stops, there are problems.'

He said, 'Rose, this isn't the time as I do want to finish that field in good weather, but before you leave us on Tuesday, you and I must have a chat about hard cash.'

I was touched and embarrassed. 'Robert, honestly, there's no need. Secretaries earn good money.'

'If you'll forgive my laying down the law, Rose, my dear, there's every need. You're my only blood relative and you've only to look around Endel to realize I can afford to help you. As I intend to. We'll go into it all, later.'

After he had gone, I said, 'June, I feel awful!'

'That's stupid,' she squeaked. 'Robert's quite right. He owes it to you to look after you as Grandfather should have done. And Robert will.'

After which I felt awful over the dark thoughts I had had about her.

The geese sleeping off their midday meal in their lean-to behind the stables, squarked drowsily as we crossed the yard to her garaged mini. 'Where does David keep his car, June?'

She gestured towards the sea-road. 'In a barn about a mile down on the right. You can't see it from here because of the curve in the road.' She stretched out her arms to the sun. 'Lovely sun! How I miss you – in winter,' she added quickly for no reason I could fathom. 'And isn't it lovely to have all Endel all to ourselves all afternoon?'

73

I glanced down at End. 'Yes. Lovely.'

In the sunshine the great windowless roof of Endel was more brown than black. The house looked more than ever like a great cat asleep in the sun. I tried to look on it with some of the affection I had for Robert. If only for his sake, I felt I should like it. I had not made up my mind about it until that moment. I didn't like Endel. And if those nocturnal steps were ghostly, Endel didn't like me.

Dolly was shut in the boot-room and scratching on the door. I asked if I could let her out. 'Or will she stray or upset the geese?'

'Not that lazy old thing after one walk today. She can sit in the sun. Let me get in the car first.'

I lugged out Dolly's basket. She climbed in with a look that made me feel like Judas Iscariot. 'Come on, Rose!' called June. 'She'll just sleep!'

We drove down the cinder road and up to the farm by the main road. Robert's car was parked outside the oast house, Murdo having used one of the farm-worker's cars to ferry the women and himself to Astead.

The oast was a tall, circular, brick building with a high-coned roof painted white and a black flying fox as a wind-vane. June jumped out. 'No sign of my lord and master? You wait, Rose. I'll go up to the top of the oast. The stairs are a bit ricketty, but I'm used to them.' She vanished, then yelled from above. 'He's just finishing the ten-acre field. As that man loves a tractor like a small boy, let's get down there fast before he decides to start on another field.'

For a pregnant woman who hated walking, she walked very fast. We charged along the sides of waterlogged fields, over narrow grass-covered stone bridges, down a built-up foot-path between ploughed fields and then along a wider and newly laid cinder track built up feet above the surrounding land.

Near the sea the wind was really strong and the incoming tide had reached the shingle. There were birds everywhere, in the rushes, overhead, along the sea-wall, and settling in great greedy clouds to pick over the newly turned heavy black soil.

I glanced back at Endel. From that distance it had lost its cat-like appearance. It was just an old house on a mound and the windows had caught the sun and sparkled.

'How maddening! The tractor's stuck! My poor Robert!' June broke into a jog-trot.

I did not follow on at once. I had spotted a small black figure wearily trundling over a field some way off. 'Dolly!' I bellowed. 'Home!'

She lifted her head as the wind carried my voice to her, but kept on stolidly.

'Rose, do hurry!' June shouted over her shoulder. 'Robert needs help!'

Robert climbed off the tractor. 'Keep on the cinder, girls,' he called and came over the field to us, in knee-high rubber boots caked in mud-clods. 'Wouldn't this have to happen on the one afternoon I've not a man within miles?'

'Darling,' wailed June, 'that tractor's stuck in the dyke wall!'

'As if I didn't know it! What's more, it's a main dyke and one that always spills over at this time of year when the tide's at flood. It'll be that in an hour and if I leave that sod of a machine where it is until I've men in the morning, it'll sink so deep half the bloody wall'll probably come away with it when we shift it out.'

'And it's your new tractor!' June looked ready to weep. 'The salt water'll ruin it!'

'Won't ruin it. Won't do it much good.' Robert smiled ruefully. 'Clearly not my day. I'm sorry about this hold-up, Rose, but this is something that can't be left. I'll go up for another tractor and see if I can drag it out alone.' He glanced at June. 'I wish you'd two good wrists, darling.'

She sighed. 'I was just thinking that. I suppose I couldn't?'

'Over my dead body,' said Robert.

I said, 'I've two good wrists.'

They looked at each other. Robert said gently, 'Thanks, Rose, but tractors aren't minis. Or have you driven one?'

'Afraid not.'

'They can be dead dodgy. It may look as if all you need do is sit up there and steer, but there's more to it than that.'

I asked, 'Couldn't you explain the more?'

'Risky.' He pushed up the peak of his tweed cap with one thumb and looked slowly all round the empty marsh. A flock of black and white curlews flapped over our heads then settled in the field to join the gulls in their search for newly turned tit-bits. 'You might manage. What do you think, June?'

'Robert darling, you're the boss!'

Something warm touched my legs. I glanced down and Dolly licked my hand, then stretched herself on her side, panting.

'What the devil are you doing here, old girl?' Robert muttered absently, looking from the tractor to June. 'I don't like the idea.'

She said, 'You won't like it if that dyke wall gives.'

I said, 'I don't imagine the salt water'll do your field any more good than it will the tractor.'

'Women! Will you twist a man's arm to get your own way! Right!' He grinned. 'I know when I'm beaten!'

It was another half-hour before the second tractor was in position and chained to the first. Robert told June to stay out of the light on the cinder track. 'I'm not ruining your elegant boots as well as all else, Rose, so I'll carry you.'

'Robert, no! I'll be much too heavy!'

'Balls,' he said smiling, and lifted me in his arms.

'Why don't you put your arms round his neck?' suggested June. 'That'll take some of your weight.'

I did as she said.

Robert said nothing until he had helped me up on to the embedded tractor. 'You aren't heavy, Rose.'

'Thanks.' I avoided looking at him. 'How does this work?'

He explained carefully all I must do. He jumped down into the mud and smiled up at me, his face flushed, his eyes gay. He looked younger and so vitally attractive that I was now having consciously to remind myself of our relationship and June's presence. Later, I realized that it was from the moment he held me in his arms that I ceased mentally to be Charles' widow and became a person in my own right again.

'All clear, Rose? Not worried?'

'Not at all! This is going to be fun!'

He said very quietly, 'You're always pretty, but now you look beautiful.'

'Thank you.' I flushed and made some excuse about the fine marsh air.

'Like the marsh?'

'Love it. I love the space and the wind in my face. My Endel blood telling, I expect.'

'You should've been a farmer's wife.' An expression that was a mixture of sadness and regret flickered over his face. He glanced back to look at June as if he also needed a reminder. 'I'm glad you like it here,' he said abruptly and walked over to the other tractor. 'Ready?' he shouted, and his voice disturbed the birds. They rose in a screaming cloud. 'We're off!'

Dolly had moved to the dyke bank. She sat bolt upright watching. I thought I heard her whimpering with cold, but it could have been the wind.

On the first two attempts the connecting chain slipped off. 'What this really needs is a bloody anchor.' Robert mopped his brow with his wrist after replacing it a second time. 'Now, let's see.'

That time the chain held. I did as Robert had instructed and had a thrill of pleasure as I felt my tractor being jerked free. I put my foot down, and being inexperienced, too rapidly. My tractor shot towards Robert's. He managed to swing his aside and the chain came adrift. Immediately, my machine went into a skid. I tried wildly to right it. I heard Dolly's frenzied barks and Robert shouting, but did not catch his words. My tractor was out of my control and after spinning in a complete circle, was sliding sideways towards the dyke. Then it started rocking. My subconscious must have remembered Bert Mercer's '... either you jumps clear or you never jumps again ...' as I had flung myself off to the left before consciously recalling his words. The tractor tilted to the right and went over as I hit the cold and surprisingly hard mud. Momentarily, I lay winded, then raised myself on an elbow and saw the huge furrow the bucket seat had ploughed out. It was now jammed in mud far more deeply than originally and the large rear wheels spun like an upturned toy.

It was then I remembered Bert Mercer.

Dolly was licking my face. I clung to her collar while I got back my breath and thought, but for a swan hitting a telegraph wire, I'd now be dead. But for – the story of my life. Shock made me smile, foolishly.

'Rose, are you all right?' Robert raced towards me, his voice rough with anxiety. 'Out of the light, Dolly!'

Dolly had been frightened, but even so her reaction startled us all. She stood across my body, her head down, ears back and hackles up, transforming her fat self into a dangerously bristling bundle of muscle. When Robert reached down to help me up, she looked at him under her eyelids, showed her teeth and gave a long, low ugly growl. Robert stepped back instinctively. June, now beside him, gasped hysterically. 'Dolly, how dare you threaten your master! Robert, you must have her destroyed! You must! Haven't I always said she's a vicious streak? She's dangerous!'

'The poor old bitch is only scared.' Robert now made no attempt to touch either Dolly or myself. 'She doesn't mean any harm. You girls can't understand what's upset her, but I do. I was a kid and she was a pup when she saw

78

one of Grandfather's men come off a tractor and break his neck in this same field years ago. This'll have brought back the memory just as it can with a horse. If you've ever tried to take a horse past a spot where he's once had a bad scare, Rose, you'll know what I'm talking about.' His voice was now very calm. 'You're not really vicious, are you, old lady?'

Dolly was still eyeing him warily, but her hackles went down as I stroked her. 'Poor Dolly. Think I was dead?'

'God alone knows,' said Robert, 'why you're not. But are you hurt?'

I smiled. 'Just muddy.'

'Just!' June clasped her hands. 'You're covered in mud! You must go straight back and have a hot bath!'

I stood up unaided, owing to Dolly. My knees were weak, but as they held me I presumed I had broken nothing. 'I'm terribly sorry to have messed things up. Can't I help get them right?'

Robert said the only way I was going to get near another tractor on his farm was by knocking him down first. 'I should never have let you up. I feel very bad about this. I even forgot to tell you to jump clear if things went wrong. What made you do that?'

I was not feeling up to explanations. 'Reflex action.'

'Thank God for it. I'm sorry about your clothes,' he apologized. 'And more than sorry about the rest.'

'It wasn't your fault. It was mine.'

'I wish you two'd stop apologizing,' put in June, 'as I'm sure you'll get pneumonia, Rose, if you don't get home and dry quickly. And if anyone thinks I'm taking that wicked animal back in my car – they can think again!'

She was very white and there were dark circles under her eyes that had not been there earlier. Robert put a soothing arm round her shoulders. 'Don't fuss, darling. If Rose feels up to driving, she can take Dolly back in mine and I'll run us both back later. I must ring round the other farms first to see if I can find some man to come out and help me right that sod.'

We walked back to the farm buildings in a subdued silence with Dolly at my heels. I was more shaken up than I cared to admit and so were the Endels. I was touched and rather surprised by the strain on their faces. Surprised, as it had been quite a time since I had had anyone to worry about me. Charles had never worried. He had said that was a wife's prerogative.

Robert gave me his car keys. Dolly flopped on to the floor at the back. I saw June's tense face in the driving mirror and was shamefully glad to be able to leave her to Robert as she appeared on the verge of real hysteria.

Dolly was so tired she was asleep directly I had rubbed her down and pulled her basket back into the boot-room. I closed the boot-room door and went in through the kitchen in my stocking feet. Every bone in my body was aching. I made up the sitting-room fire before going up. The hall telephone rang as I was running my bath.

It was June. 'Don't wait tea. Help yourself, as we'll be a little later than we thought. That stupid match seems to have cleared the marsh of able-bodied men and the only available man with proper lifting tackle can't come out from Coxden until he finishes the job he's now working on. I did suggest our nipping back for tea, but as Robert says, if we leave, ten to one that's when he'll turn up. You'll be all right on your own?'

'Fine, thanks. I just feel so guilty to give all this extra bother.'

'That's stupid,' she squeaked, and rang off.

I lowered the receiver slowly as the realization that I was alone in Endel, hit me. I wished I dared bring Dolly into the sitting-room, but had put up enough blacks for the afternoon without adding to them.

The house was very quiet. The chugging of the Monster had a companionable sound. It was still light outside and the others were bound to be back before dark. All the same, I sang far too loudly in my bath.

CHAPTER SEVEN

It was a unique opportunity to look at my ancestors' portraits at my leisure. I didn't feel strong enough to take it,
but kept up my self-respect with the reflection that the light
wouldn't be good enough.

I took a tea-tray into the sitting-room, closed the door,
switched on all the lights, got the fire blazing and put my
feet up on the sofa. My bath, the tea and the warmth of
the room soothed me into a gentle coma in which my latest
escape from a peculiarly messy death seemed only mildly
amusing. Yet, had I been killed, the marsh would have
converted one more purely accidental death into additional
proof of the Endel legend. Thus, I thought pompously, do
legends arise.

I thought of Robert, decided that was folly, and thought
of David as an antidote. Then I remembered Dolly at his
cottage this morning and that I was now alone in Endel. I
needed another antidote and belatedly remembered Adrian.
He had vanished from my mind as totally as friends made
on a holiday usually did. I recalled his face with difficulty
and a sense of guilt. Had he not talked sense into me,
almost certainly I would have refused Robert's invitation.

That brought me back to Robert again. I did not want to
think about him. I even tried kidding myself I wished
Adrian had not given me that good advice. It was no use.
Robert's face floated through my mind. Robert smiling. I
closed my eyes and fell asleep, smiling.

I had no idea how long I slept, or when I woke,
momentarily, where I was. It was dark enough for the
middle of the night. Then I saw the glowing white ash in
the hearth. I got off the sofa to chuck on more wood and
switch on the light, forgetting I had left it on. It was only
when I touched the switch that I noticed the chugging had

stopped. 'Oh, God, no! Not again!' I exclaimed aloud.

The fire was picking up. I held my watch to it. Half past six. The others were so late, they must now be back at any minute. Since I hadn't been shown how to switch over to the emergency supply, or for that matter, been down to the cellars at all, all I could do was all I actually wanted to do – and that was sit tight by the warm fire.

That was fine, until I discovered there were only two small logs left in the hearth box that had not been replenished since Murdo went off at noon.

The wood was stored in one of the cellars, the candles and matches were kept somewhere in the pantry. I did not know precisely where, as June had talked of showing me but had not yet done so. I imagined they would be easy to find and once I had a light I could collect Dolly and take her with me to get the wood. I didn't relish the idea, but I could not let the others return to an icy as well as dark house. Then I remembered the hall fire had not been lit that day and the hall log-chest would be full.

Background heat in the hall was provided by electric strips fitted to the ceiling beams and from the chill in the hall air, the Monster had failed within minutes of my dropping off. I left the sitting-room door open to give me some light. It shut itself as I crossed the hall and the darkness was a smothering blanket. Having always lived in places where light could be obtained by touching a switch, I was appalled by my own helplessness. It was about a minute before my eyes even began to adjust themselves and a minute I did not enjoy. As a child I had been scared by blind man's buff, but even then one could see some light through the bandage.

A board behind me creaked and I started as if shot. Another creaked. Then another. Obviously the changed temperature warping the boards. Obviously or not, I moved on too quickly and then hit my head on something round and hard. My hands identified the object as the high pedestal table that stood by the wall on the left of the stairs and in the opposite direction from the log-chest. My head hurt and the impact had not helped my nerves, but the table was a landmark. I groped round it, found the stairs and sat on the bottom step rubbing my head and wishing I had a torch. Being so softened by civilization, it had not occurred to me that a pocket torch in an isolated country house could be as essential to comfortable living as a toothbrush. There must be torches in Endel. There was probably one in the pantry. All I had to do was find the swing door. That should be no problem as it was now on my left and if I used the wall as a guide, I couldn't miss it.

I stood up – and a board creaked on the first landing. Then a series creaked, the creaks were slow and regular as footsteps – and I recognized them. I did not mean to sit down again and hold my breath. I just did that.

The footsteps had reached the head of the stairs. They paused, then moved on along the landing. I breathed out, told myself to stop acting like a moron and to get on with the business of finding the pantry. But I wasn't listening properly to myself. I was too busy listening to those foot-steps.

They were coming back to the stair-head. They were even more clearly footsteps than in my room at night. I began to shake. The cold, the darkness, the lingering effects of my fall and the thought of Robert's birth night, had combined to skim off my civilized veneer as successfully as Murdo skinned the rabbits he shot for Dolly.

Again the steps paused at the head of the stairs. Then, as I was sitting on them, I felt the slight vibration with the next creak. Someone – something – was on the stairs and coming down.

Up to that moment I had never imagined I could be made hysterical. Frightened or desperate, yes, but not hysterical. Not, until I had consciously to fight against the desire to scream and experienced the surge of senseless panic that literally gripped my throat, tightened my chest, made my heart seem too big for my rib-cage and my mouth dry as sandpaper.

My reason went out of the window. I leapt off the stairs and through the darkness and fumbled the wall, sobbing with relief as I felt the outline of a door. My sweaty hand slithered on the knob and I was through the door and had slammed it after me before I realized it was not the swing door. The colder air and the new formal shapes of the shadows proved I was in the drawing-room. The one room in Endel in which I shivered even when the sun shone.

I didn't dare stay there; I didn't dare go back to the hall. I pressed myself against the door, gibbering with unreasoning and purely primitive fear. Very plainly, I heard the steps coming down into the hall, then going back up the stairs and growing fainter along the landing. They did not return. The house was silent.

On oath, I could not have said how long it was before the silence was shattered by Dolly barking, outside the house. I opened the door. 'Dolly! Where are you?' My voice came out as a June-type squeak. 'How'd you get out?'

The sound of the front door opening nearly pushed me back over the edge. 'Who's that?'

'David.' I saw his outline before a torch beam blinded me. 'What's going on? Apart from the Monster's obviously packing up again? What are you doing up against that wall?'

I could not answer. I forgot everything beyond his being a fellow human with a light and Dolly. She did not growl when he rushed at me. She sat on my feet when he held me in his arms. I rested my head on his shoulder and after a time stopped breathing in gasps.

'What ails you, love?' He stroked my hair as if I were a child. 'Ghoulies and ghosties and long-legged beasties and things that go bump in the night? Or are you just allergic to being alone in the dark? And if you're alone, why are you alone?'

84

I now could, but didn't answer, at once. Sanity and memory were returning and my cheek was against the wooden button of a duffle-coat. 'David, what're you doing?'

'If you've to ask that, you've been a widow too long.'

'Not now. Before. Why're you here?'

'I'm just back from London. Dolly came to meet me and seemed in a right state and as I saw the lights out up here, I thought I'd better investigate.'

'Why?'

'Public-spirited citizen. Endel could've been being burgled. It will be, one of these fine days, as it's packed with the loot of ages and Robert refuses to lock doors. Don't ask me why. No doubt he knows his own business and neighbours. Just tell me why you're still all of a tremble. What happened?'

'It'll sound so silly.'

'I like silly stories.'

'You'll think I'm sick.'

'And why should what I think worry you?' He tightened his hold. 'See here, Rose,' he said with a kindness that I would not previously have thought him capable of possessing, 'I realize you scarcely know me, that you don't like me, partly as I remind you of your late husband, partly as you just don't like me. So what? No one can like everyone. But clearly something has nearly scared the living daylights out of you, and the fact that I don't happen to be your dish is no reason for your not telling me what it was. If you want me to keep it quiet, I will. If you want me to tell the Endels, I'll do just that. Who knows? I may even be able to help, if only by being a pair of ears. So?'

It would have been a relief to talk, had that duffle-coat not throttled me. I had now remembered the time gap between those steps fading and Dolly's barks. He could have got out of the house and round to the front. He could have chosen very carefully to make his official appearance at the precise moment he had. He could have guessed my resistance would then be at zero. He could have been in his

85

cottage that morning.

I tried to move away, but his hold was too firm. I said, 'I'm really all right now, thanks. I just dozed off and woke up in the dark. I was a bit confused. All I need now is some light. Thanks for lending me your shoulder.' I hesitated. 'You're only vaguely like Charles.'

I felt him stiffen. 'Like to bet?' He kissed my mouth hard. He kissed well. 'You did say, vaguely?'

I said nothing.

He said, 'If there's one thing that annoys me more than someone with brains who doesn't bother to use 'em, it's a submissive woman.' He let me go. 'I'll see if I can get on the emergency plant.'

He did not have to do that. A pair of headlights had swung past the open front door. Dolly crept out of the hall. Five minutes later Robert had the emergency machine going. It took him another ten to repair the minor fuse that had blown in a major part of the Monster. He said, 'What we all need now, is a drink.'

June told David about my fall. 'Poor Rose! What an afternoon and evening!'

Robert sat on the arm of my chair. 'I do hope you weren't too upset by the lack of lights?'

David answered for me. 'Not your cousin Rose! Nothing she enjoys more than floundering round in the dark! Isn't that so, Rose?'

I said, 'I was a bit confused, being sleepy.'

June said, 'What I don't follow is how you came to be in on it, David?'

'I came in through your front door.' He gave her the explanation he had given me. Robert asked, apparently casually, 'How'd Dolly get out? Didn't you shut her in the boot-room, Rose?'

'Yes.' Our eyes met. 'Can she open the door?'

'Not to my knowledge, though it wouldn't be beyond her to push up the latch with her muzzle. She's a crafty old bitch. Well!' Robert stood up. 'Junie, if we're dining out,

86

we ought to get changed. Or do you think Rose has had too hectic a day to feel up to an outing? She'll be far too polite to say so herself.'

'Poor Rose, you are so pale!' June flapped her eyelashes anxiously. 'Perhaps we should stay in. Can you cancel the table, darling?'

'Easily.' Robert glanced from June to David. 'How about joining us for a scratch supper, David?'

June looked as displeased and surprised as I felt when David said if Robert was sure it would not be too much trouble for June, there was nothing he'd like more. June had to say, 'Good. We'll have a little party.'

'Suits me.' David got off the sofa. 'Are you ladies going to insist I remain in my gents natty suiting, or can I slip into something more comfortable?'

'Anything you like, David.' Now, June sounded as tired as I felt.

'That go for you, Rose?'

'Sure.' I met David's eyes. 'I don't give a damn.'

Behind his shoulder Robert caught my eye and smiled slightly and privately. I had not a bone or muscle that wasn't aching and my nerves could have been much more healthy, but suddenly I stopped feeling tired.

David was away about an hour. June spent the time fussing as if forty not one extra guest, were expected. At supper, the two men did most of the talking and most of the talk was on football. The Marsh Villages had won the match. Robert was due to collect five pounds from some Astead friend. David had lost ten bob to Murdo. 'Think he'll be sober enough to remember it when he gets in to-night, Robert?'

'Ever met the Scotsman who was too drunk to remember the man who owes him money? He'll—' Robert broke off as we all heard the rumble in the distance. 'God Almighty! What was that?'

'Sounded like blasting down by the sea-wall.' David put down his fork. 'No one's doing any round here, are they?'

'They'd better not with the wind that's getting up and the sea high.' Robert went out to the front door. 'Can't see anything,' he called back, 'but I can smell – what? Anthracite! David! Have you lit your boiler?' he added urgently.

'Yes. Just now, to get a bath tonight.' David left the table. 'You think that came from End?'

'Came from your direction. We'd better find out. Keep the sweet, June! If that was David's boiler, we may have a fire on our hands!'

June buried her face in her hands as the men ran out of Endel. 'This is too much! Honestly, Rose, I try not to grumble as Robert so loves the country, but if ever progress has missed out on any place, this is it! If it isn't the Monster, it's the ball-cock! If it's not the ball-cock, it's the plant up at the farm! Or the telephones! Or tiles off the roof! And if it's now the boiler down at End, as that's the only way of heating the water down here, you realize what'll have to happen?'

'David'll have to stay here?'

'Where else? On a Saturday night out of season. There are no hotels open this side of Astead. He's our tenant. He's paid his rent in advance. If his cottage is uninhabitable, we'll have to offer temporary accommodation.'

I could have wept with her. 'If it was his boiler blowing, how long before it can be mended?'

'If it wasn't the weekend, not more than a day or two. Robert may be able to coax someone out to look at it tomorrow, but they won't start work until Monday at the earliest. Oh dear. I don't want to sound selfish, but we've so enjoyed having you to ourselves this afternoon. This means he'll be with us most of your visit.'

I thought suddenly of that tractor and how one afternoon could have been the sole time my cousins had me to themselves. Then I thought of what had happened later, including the hour David had spent in his cottage.

June grumbled on. 'Without the boiler to heat the water,

Robert'll insist on draining the tank in the roof to prevent its freezing tonight. As it's the end of January, it's bound to freeze. Robert won't want a burst tank and the ceiling down to add to what's gone already. Oh, damn David!'

I said more to placate myself than her. 'We can't be sure yet it was his boiler?'

'What else could it be – in that direction?' She was very peeved. 'If it is – and I'm sure it is – though I may be mis-judging him terribly, I wouldn't put it past him to have done this on purpose to force us into letting him stay here with you. He has got a yen for you. You know I thought so be-fore. Now, I'm certain. I've been watching him. He hasn't taken his eyes off you once all evening. Haven't you noticed?'

'No,' I said untruthfully.

The telephone was ringing. June wore an aura of gloomy triumph when she returned from taking the call. 'That was Robert from the cottage. I was right! I'll be right about the rest, you bet!'

My wine glass was nearly full. I knocked it back in one go, but it did not make any difference.

Later that night I was in my room, but still dressed when someone knocked quietly. 'It's Robert, Rose. May I come in?' He had to wait while I unlocked the door. 'I'm glad you've done that.'

'I thought you didn't approve of locked doors?'

'In general, I don't. This is rather an exceptional occa-sion – in more ways than one.' He came in and leant against the closed door. His expression made me feel as much of a heel as he so plainly did. At the same time I managed to feel wonderful. It was a feeling I had forgotten and so pleasant I nearly forgot the other.

'Why are you here, Robert?'

'June asked me to talk to you on the quiet.' He looked at his feet. 'She's more than somewhat het-up. It could just be her physiological condition, but she doesn't normally get bees in her bonnet without fairly good cause. She's now got one about David.' He looked up then. 'She says she's warned you he's fixated on you, but she can't get you to take her seriously. From your locking your door I'd say possibly she's misjudged you. Right?'

I sat on the edge of the writing desk. 'It's not so much June – or maybe it is – I don't know. I haven't got David's number.'

'Does he disturb you?'

'If by that you mean does he make me feel uneasy, yes.'

'Because he's so obviously attracted to you?'

I said, 'That's no compliment, Robert.'

He put his hands in his pockets and jingled their contents. 'Perhaps he's no more than a harmless nut.'

'Only perhaps?'

He said slowly, 'I have to leave it there as I don't know the right answer. I do know that a kind of pattern seems to be shaping. Twice my machine's packed up when it shouldn't. Now his boiler's done the same. All coincidences? Possibly. But coincidence has to stop somewhere, so tonight I'm breaking my rule, locking every door that has a key and removing the keys. I shall do that as long as he's in Endel. If he asks why, I'll blame the gale that's now blowing up. It's going to be a good 'un by the way the glass is behaving.'

'I see. Robert, could he have blown his boiler?'

'Easily. Jam the flue with a bit of brick or slate and the moment it had worked up enough steam it'ld have to blow.'

'It couldn't have been an accident?'

'Oh, yes.' He smiled ruefully. 'It's an old building. In any old building there are loose bricks in the chimneys. One could have slipped down. Not even an expert could prove otherwise. Whatever, or whoever caused it, the effect's been chaotic. The front of the boiler and half the chimney are now all over his living-room as it blew out not up.'

'Then if you hadn't asked him to supper, he could have been hurt?'

'Rose, we had asked him to supper. He knew he was

90

going to be out when he went back and lit it. Of course, that could be another coincidence.'

I said, 'A lucky one, for him.'

'Very.' He was quiet for a few seconds. 'I said I'd never had cause to regret having him as a tenant. This'll teach me to keep my big mouth shut. I know I can't prove he's mucking up my property, but there's no question that he's upset June badly and I can see how he's upsetting you. I'd like to kick him out here and now, but how can I? I've not one suspicion that'ld hold up in law and he's got the brains to know it. So all I can do is keep a close eye on him myself and beg you, particularly, to be on your guard and tell me at once and any time, anything you think I ought to know about his future behaviour. Will you do that?' He came closer and was about to touch me when he remembered and replaced his hands in his pockets. 'For June's peace of mind as much as my own?'

I just nodded. I wanted to talk. I wanted to tell him all about this evening. I didn't dare risk it. If I said anything I would say too much and so would he. He was June's husband. I was her guest. June might not believe it – wives seldom did – but in common with far more women than is generally assumed, I regarded other women's husbands as other women's property. I wanted a mink coat. I wouldn't steal for one. I wanted Robert to kiss me now as much as every instinct I possessed told me he wanted to kiss me. David wasn't the only man in Endel against whom I now had to guard, and June was probably the only person in the house who did not know it. David did. All evening he had been watching Robert and myself as closely as June had been watching him.

Robert backed to the door. 'One can see David's angle, unfortunately. He wants to be near you. He wants to touch you. He wants you.' He compressed his lips to a straight line. 'One can sympathize with, if not approve of, his behaviour. 'Night, Rose.'

I heard him knock on the guest-room door. 'Got all you

want, David? Is there a key on the inside of this door? Turn it tonight, mate. I've just advised Rose to do the same. We're in for one hell of a gale.'

I relocked my own door and began to breathe more normally after a few minutes.

CHAPTER EIGHT

The gale reached full force in the small hours. It screamed round the house, howled down the corridors, rattled every door and window, lifted every loose floorboard. If there were any footsteps, they were drowned in the uproar. Endel shook as if in the hands of a giant gone mad and the loose tiles flying off the roof hit the yard below with the crack of rifle fire.

There was a new moon that night. The slither of light kept appearing between the thin, scurrying clouds. The noise made sleep impossible. Wrapped in my quilt, I watched fascinated from my window, standing a little back from the shaking leaded panes.

The tide had come in again. Wave after wave crashed over the top of the Midstreet Wall, flinging up thousands of pebbles to crash on the sea-road. When the road was flooded the wind flicked up miniature waves on the surface.

A door below started banging. Then a new and very faint sound was added to the thundering elemental chorus. I searched the yard from both windows wondering what had set off the geese. It was no night for a wandering tramp. Murdo was away in Astead, David in the guest-room along the corridor. I had been awake hours. I hadn't heard anyone on the stairs and that was not merely because of the wind as a few minutes later I clearly heard someone going down. I saw no one in the yard, but heard Robert's voice calling Dolly in. The geese shouted again. About fifteen minutes later I heard Robert coming back up and switching off lights on his way.

I went back to bed and at last, to sleep. I woke much later than usual to a strange stillness. The gale had blown itself out. The marsh was littered with shingle, torn-up scrubs and rushes, and the yard was strewn with broken tiles.

Breakfast was at nine as it was Sunday. Robert was out when I joined June. Her face was pale and puffy. David came down a few minutes after myself. He wore his grey roll-neck sweater and brown cords. 'Anyone get any sleep?'

'Some.' I passed him the tea June had poured. 'How about you, June?'

'I don't mind wind, just the headache it always gives me.'

'Can I get you anything for it?'

'Thanks, Rose. I've had a couple of tablets.' She roused herself with a patent effort. 'Do help yourselves from the sideboard.'

David raised one silver cover. 'Ham, Rose?'

'Just toast, thanks.'

'Marmalade or honey?' He offered both as if my choice were of vital importance to him. June caught my eye. 'Aren't I right?' was written all over her face.

'Robert up at the farm?' asked David, sitting down beside me.

'No. There's a job he had to do here.' June glanced at me queerly. 'He won't be long. And you haven't told us how you slept, David?'

'Not too badly. I rather enjoy the sound of wind, so long as it's not my property it's heaving around.' He smiled at me. 'That's right, love. Egocentric bastard, that's me.'

Robert was twenty minutes late. His face was hard and his eyes angry. His expression softened so instantly when he looked at me that June must have noticed had she not rushed out to the kitchen for his porridge. David noticed. 'Chores done, Robert?'

'Yes.' Robert sat at the head of the table. 'And a sod of a chore it was!'

I forgot David. 'Something wrong, Robert?'

He breathed deeply. 'I don't want to tell you, but you'll have to know, so I'll give it to you straight. I've just buried Dolly.'

My hands flew to my face. 'Oh, no!'

'I'm sorry. Yes. The boot-room door burst open in the night. She went into the yard. A tile must have hit her. I found her dead when I got down to shut the door in the night. I couldn't do anything for her, so I put her in her basket till this morning.' His eyes caressed me kindly. 'I'm more sorry than I can say. That old bitch has been a part of my life for fourteen years and I know how fond you got of her in the short time you've known her.' June was back. He said, 'They know about Dolly, darling.'

David asked quietly, 'Where did the tile get her?'

Robert said, 'You can have the details later away from the breakfast table and the girls.'

'Sorry.' David polished his glasses, and blinked at us with narrowed blue eyes. 'I'm sorry about old Dolly. She was a nice dog.'

'She'd a good long life.' Robert handed my cup to June to refill. 'That's something to remember now.'

June said petulantly, 'She was only a dog. You English seem to forget that.'

We all looked at her and no more was said about Dolly. No more was said about anything for the rest of breakfast.

June spent most of that morning lying down. At Robert's suggestion I went with him and David to clear up End Cottage. The living-room looked as if hit by a hurricane.

Robert pointed out a crack in the chimney wall. 'Something must have blocked the flue behind here. I'm sorry your books are in such a mess, David, but as your landlord I'm relieved it blew out, not up. I had this roof repaired just before you moved in and the bill still makes me wince.' He surveyed the soot-scattered room. 'Many books ruined?'

I helped David stack them. He said, 'Could be worse.

Most'll clean off once they're dry.'

I asked, 'Where's the water from?'

They showed me the broken water pipe. It ran up in the chimney to the tank in the attic. They had drained it, last night. 'Luckily,' said David, 'as I'd been away, it wasn't too full.'

Robert spun round from examining the chimney wall. 'You didn't light the boiler without pumping up first?'

'No. I pumped some up. Think I didn't pump enough and hence this? If so, you'd better send me the bill when you get it.'

'No need of that, thanks. This is structural, my responsibility, and I'm covered. But the insurance blokes may ask awkward questions.'

'Christ,' said David, 'they always do.'

Robert wanted to get up on the roof. 'Come and help me get a ladder, David. You'll be all right on your todd, Rose?'

'Quite. There are hundreds of these books still to sort. How many've you got, David?'

'Here? About four hundred. I've more in my flat.' He smiled down at me. 'A man without a woman has to do something on the long marsh evenings.'

'Let's get that ladder,' said Robert. 'I've still a farm to see to.'

Two-thirds of the books were paperbacks and most of the rest textbooks. The selection of novels surprised me by containing as many classics as moderns.

One of Charles' pet sayings floated through my mind. 'One can learn far more about people by seeing with which books they choose to live than by seeing them nude. The latter remains a covering; the former exposes the mind.'

Charles, I thought. I could hear his clipped, rather affected voice. I thought on him hard and for the first time, without wincing. Somewhere the bells must be going ring-a-ding-ding – but not for me. For Robert.

I must not think of Robert. I had to concentrate on something else, anything else. So what kind of a mind did those books expose?

Oddly, reluctantly, I grew genuinely interested in the problem. I sorted Tolstoy, Chekhov, Jane Austen, Proust, D.H.L., Joyce. I sorted rows of living novelists some of whom I had read, all of whom I recognized as officially 'serious'. There were a few Chandler-type thrillers. There was no obvious pornography. There was no book that could not be had for the taking in any good public library. The whole collection looked to have been compiled with affection and care and even some of the paperbacks were ten years old. Clearly, he loved books. Would anyone who loved books deliberately damage them?

I sat back and had another look round. I thought of Dolly sniffing at this cottage doorstep this time yesterday. If it had been David whom she had then scented, why had he waited until last night to fix his boiler? Was that important? Or was it futile to try and fathom the workings of a sick man, unless one was a psychiatrist?

I looked down at the books. Did their choice really expose a sick mind?

I opened one after another. I was not looking for anything in particular. I noticed David's name on the flyleaf of book after book. Some were just marked with his initials and nearly all with what I took to be the date of purchase. A few were presents. 'David, from Gillian.' 'Dave, from Harry.'

One large and obviously expensive textbook had a longer inscription in a neat Italic handwriting.

'To my Godson and nephew, David Gairlie Lofthouse, on the occasion of his twentieth birthday with affectionate good wishes from his Godfather and Uncle,

Kenneth S. Gairlie.'

I read that a couple of times, at first incuriously and then with genuine curiosity. I couldn't explain that to myself. I put the book down, then instantly picked it up again and had another look at the flyleaf.

Something about that rang a bell. I was still trying to place it when a real bell rang. By the time I had traced that one to the telephone in the one bedroom upstairs, the former had slipped my mind.

'Rose,' demanded June, 'what are you all doing?'

I explained. 'If you want Robert,' I added peering out of the very low window, 'he's just coming down the cinder road with a ladder and David.'

'Don't bother to call him. Just tell him I've managed to get hold of Yates, the builder, and he's coming out to look at End after church. That'll be twelve-thirty-ish. Will you tell Robert that if he wants to get up to the farm this morning, he's only got an hour left.'

'Sure. How's the head?'

'Better. I'm just praying the wind doesn't come back.'

'Robert says the glass is rising.'

'Huh. If it goes up too fast,' she said glumly, 'we'll have a mist. How's the clearing going?'

'Still quite a lot to do.'

'I don't imagine David's shedding any tears now he's got you down there,' she said, and rang off.

I went outside and handed on her message. Robert said he'd just nip up the ladder for a quick look round and then get up to the farm. 'As my foreman's come in with one of the other blokes, what I want to do up there won't take long.' He had his look at the roof and came down. David was holding the ladder. 'No damage up top I could see. I'll be off. Coming along for the ride, Rose?'

'What on?' queried David casually. 'Another tractor?'

Robert's face tightened, but he kept his tone equally casual. 'Not on the Sabbath, chum, unless we're harvesting. Offends the neighbours. Why don't you come along too?'

'What as?' drawled David. 'Chaperon? Alibi? Or both?'

There was a very faint, very loud, silence. The two men just looked at each other. Then Robert smiled – with his lips. 'Take your pick, chum. Or stay here and finish up here, then go back to Endel and have a drink with June and we'll join you there. Coming, Rose?'

'Before you wrench her from me,' said David before I could say anything, 'as I take it you'll be using your estate car, will you lend me the mini?'

'What for?' Robert raised his eyebrows.

'To run all these books up to the house to dry off.'

'Where's your car?'

'Astead. The bloody dynamo's burnt out. It got me as far as Astead on Friday, then died on me. I dumped it at that garage just beyond the station and went on by train. I couldn't collect it yesterday as my train didn't get in until five to six and the place shuts at five-thirty. Rose's pal drove me out.'

'Whom?' asked Robert tersely.

'A large man called Bert. Asked real kindly after the pretty little lady, he did, and I said the little lady was doing fine, not knowing she had spent the afternoon dicing with death on one of your tractors. Incidentally, Rose, he sent you his regards.'

'Thanks.' I explained Bert Mercer to Robert in more detail. 'If I did dice with death yesterday afternoon, he's the main reason death lost out.'

'Well, well,' said Robert with a smile that did reach his eyes, 'I must remember to give Bert Mercer the tip he has coming to him next time I need a taxi. I must get on now. You're coming with me, Rose? Do. I never had time to show you round properly, yesterday.'

David said as he'd never been shown round the farm properly, he might as well come too.

'Thought you wanted to borrow the mini?'

'Changed my mind, Robert. Any objections? How about you, Rose?'

I said, 'Robert's my host. Up to him. I'm just going along for the ride.'

'My God,' grumbled Robert, 'either come or stay, man!

The time you egg-heads waste in talk! Do you ever do anything else, David?'

'Frequently.' We all walked quickly up the cinder road towards the garages. 'Mostly we do what we're paid to do.'

'What's that?' grunted my cousin. 'Muck about in labs?'

'That too. It's not the main. In the main we're paid – to think.'

'Some people have it easy.' Robert dodged round me as we reached the yard. 'Don't look at the boot-room, Rose,' he said in a different tone. 'Only way to deal with it. Look the other way.'

I took his advice. David looked very deliberately at the closed boot-room door.

We did not have time to get round the farm. Robert barely had time to exchange a few words with his foreman before June rang to say Mr Yates had arrived. He had slipped out before the sermon. 'No offence to the vicar, but I reckon I've heard it all before and Mrs. Endel said it was urgent. Well, then, let's take a look at it.'

He was a small, sturdy youngish man with a fair-skinned square face and calm eyes. He wore a dark blue suit, regimental tie and his shoes had a blinding polish. When he disappeared with Robert and David to inspect the damage, June told me he had been a regular soldier and was now a master builder. He came from Coxden.

She was in a tiz until they returned. 'When can you start work, Mr Yates?'

'Tuesday morning, Mrs Endel.' He accepted a glass of beer. 'I can't spare men tomorrow, but I'll have them down at End first thing Tuesday morning.'

'A long job, Mr Yates?' asked David.

'I'd be a liar if I said I could answer that afore I've seen the full extent of the damage, Mr Lofthouse.' Mr Yates had a gentle broad-vowelled Coxden voice. He looked tough enough to build Endel single-handed. 'Like I was saying earlier, it'll depend on your main stack. All these old marsh cottages get their strength from their main stacks. If you've damaged that, then there's no saying where it'll end. If not, it's a short job. It'ld be the same if you damaged your main beam up there, Mr Endel.' He looked up and traced the beam with a pointed finger. 'That's your main running between your two main stacks. This building is too heavy to be supported by the one, so they balanced it on the two. But it's that beam that gives it its strength.' He walked the length of the hall under the great beam. 'Lovely bit of timber. Don't see many this length these days.'

I asked, 'Is that really holding up this house?'

'That's just what it's doing, madam. You see those cross-beams above? They're holding up the first floor. Those above hold the next floor, above them the attics and the roof. But the lot rest on this main beam. Long as this beam holds steady, Endel'll hold steady.' He peered up again, frowning. 'See you've been fixing up some more of your electric wires, Mr Endel.'

'A few more.' Robert put down his glass on the pedestal table. 'You'll bring out the new boiler?'

'I'll arrange for the stove and fittings tomorrow. We'll bring 'em with us, Tuesday, and if the stack's undamaged Mr Lofthouse should be back in his cottage Wednesday evening.' He turned to David. 'You'll be staying here till then?'

David smiled apologetically at June. 'If I can continue to impose on Mrs Endel?'

Robert answered for her. 'Naturally you'll stay here. We've more than enough room.'

'That's a fact, Mr Endel.' Mr Yates finished his beer. 'There's not many private houses this size still in use as such in these parts. Lovely old place you got here. The men that built it knew all there was to know about building on marsh. Reckon last night's gale didn't trouble you much?'

June looked at the floor. Robert glanced at me. David watched Robert and myself as he had been doing the entire morning. Robert said, 'We'd a few tiles off the roof.'

'If a Force Nine gale can't do worse to a building that's

100

been standing four hundred years, there's not much wrong with the building. Mind you, Mr Endel, and no offence intended,' went on the builder, 'but if you're thinking of making any more alterations, you'd best take it softly, softly, as we used to say when I was soldiering.' He listened to the gentle thud of the Monster. 'There's not much vibration up here from that machine you got down there and I don't say what there is below is enough to do any real damage to the foundations, though I'd not fancy to commit myself on that. You best keep an eye out for that. These old buildings can stand a lot, but they can't stand what they weren't put up to stand and the men as built your foundations weren't thinking of electricity. You'll have allowed for that?'

'Of course.'

The conversation grew technical. I lost the thread long before Robert offered to show Mr Yates his latest improvements to the Monster. David went down with them.

June began fussing about lunch.

We were having a cold chicken cooked yesterday by Mrs Hodges, a salad, an apple pie that only needed putting in the oven, and fresh cream that needed whisking. I offered to see to the pie, cream and lay the table.

'I'll show you what we'll need.' She swept me into the kitchen and shut the door. 'Wednesday!'

'Only three days.' I took the pie out of the fridge. 'Which is the hot oven and can this dish stand sudden heat?'

'Yes. The one on the left.' She touched my arm. 'Must you go on Tuesday? Can't you stay until next weekend? At least that way we'll have you to ourselves for some time after David's gone.'

She sounded so sincere I nearly dropped the pie. I put it in and closed the oven door. 'It's sweet of you, June, but I should be thinking of my next job. May I come down for another weekend, later?'

'It's David! Isn't it?' She sat on the kitchen table. 'He's spoilt Endel for you! I knew he would!' Her voice had a hint of yesterday's hysteria. 'I told Robert! I've never liked him – I said that long before you came or we even knew there was any chance you'd come. I know he's had a bad time – I'm sorry for him – but I just don't trust him. I've been telling Robert that ever since he rented him End! But you know what men are and how they will stick together! Robert kept saying David couldn't help being odd after being blown up and goodness only knows what and that there was no real vice in him. He's always said the same about Dolly – and you saw how her vicious streak came out yesterday! Robert's so kind himself, he just judges every-one and everything by his own standards! Even this morn-ing after Dolly – he still insists it could just have been an accident. An accident!' she repeated shrilly. 'One blow on the head – maybe. But her head was bashed right in. Robert says she looked exactly as if someone had gone for her and gone berserk. And though he looked, he couldn't find the tile that hit her. He said it must have been covered with blood and hair, but he couldn't find it.' Suddenly, she clapped a hand over her mouth. 'Oh! Robert said I mustn't tell you! He said it wasn't fair to frighten you, as she could've died accidentally, and anyway no one could possibly prove even if she didn't, that David's responsible.' Her eyes were nearly popping out of her head. 'You won't tell Robert I've told you?'

I had to sit down fast. 'No. No. June, are you sure about this?'

'So sure, it made me vomit! Robert told me after break-fast. Till then, I thought like you – just a tile by accident. Robert says that's impossible – and she hadn't put up a fight. It must've been someone she trusted. Murdo's still away – it must be David!'

I thought of Dolly on the defensive yesterday. 'She'd have gone for a stranger. '

'Of course, she would! As Robert says – would he him-self harm her after keeping her so long after Grandfather? Everyone knows I won't go near a dog – and you wouldn't hurt her! Robert says you wouldn't have had the physical strength to do what was done. David has.'

I said mechanically. 'He's got powerful shoulders. But, June, he loved Dolly. And she loved him. He wouldn't!'

'No? You've seen his cottage. I haven't. Robert says he's ruined dozens of his books. Isn't he meant to love books?'

I nodded dumbly, thinking now of Robert's theory of a certain pattern shaping. The books. Dolly. And next?

June voiced the words my mind refused to frame. 'I wish he wasn't so obviously gone on you. Perhaps you're wise to want to leave us on Tuesday.' She got off the table as we heard the men returning up the cellar stairs. 'We'll look after you, Rose. I promise you. Just be very careful to keep out of his way and if he tries to get you to himself for any reason, make some excuse and tell Robert. Robert hasn't said so,' she added in a conspiratorial whisper, 'as I know he doesn't want to upset me because of the baby or frighten you, but he is a little worried now. I've noticed he's determined not to let you out of his sight while David's around. Haven't you?'

'Now you point it out,' I agreed untruthfully.

'He'll see you're safe. He's so clever! Then, after David's lease ends, you must come down for a longer and happier visit. Will you, dear?'

Her attitude appalled me as much as her news. Could any woman be so blind about the man she loved? Then I remembered myself when I first met Charles. Love didn't only blind, it could sap the intelligence, douse the instincts. Momentarily and intentionally, I dwelt on the thought of Robert. I was such a lousy judge of men. Could I be as wrong about him as I'd been about Charles? I didn't know the answer. I did know one thing. I had disliked and distrusted David from our first meeting. I hadn't then known he was a sick man with an ugly temper. I knew it now – and Dolly was dead.

CHAPTER NINE

Lunch was even more atmospheric than breakfast. We all seemed to be watching each other and waiting for anticipated conversational cues to which could be made anticipated replies. It reminded me of one of the formal all-female lunches in Spain to which I had often been invited by Spanish friends while Charles was working. We had all sat round watching our waistlines and taking it in turns to sigh over the sadness of a woman's lot, indigestion, the pains of labour and the impossibility of outbidding the American service wives for servants. Sooner or later someone always announced, 'We are here to suffer.' Someone else then made the correct reply. 'We shall be happier in Paradise.'

June would have been absolutely at home at those luncheon-parties. The chicken was too tough; the apples were too tart; Mr Yates was bound to overload his bill; Murdo was certain to be incapable of good work tomorrow owing to the monumental hangover with which he would return tonight.

David said, 'At least it's a glorious day. Warm enough for spring.'

'Too warm,' retorted June. 'We'll get a mist.'

Robert managed to catch my eye. That was no simple matter as I was consciously avoiding looking at him. 'I've press-ganged David into lending me a hand at the farm this afternoon. I won't ask you along, Rose, as we'll be toting fodder bales. What are you girls going to do? Retire with the Sunday papers?'

June said she thought that a lovely idea. I kept my views to myself until the men had gone. 'Would you mind if I took a walk? I feel I must have air.'

'Oh my word, you are an energetic body! You really

Endel. A man of Midstreet. Born, 17 January 1885. Died 8 August 1966.

I moved on. Maria Ellen Endel, beloved wife of Robert Endel, Esq., of Endel House. Another move. Hélène Monique Endel, beloved wife of Richard Endel, Esq. Aged 19.

Roberta Endel, daughter of ... Martha Endel, wife of ... Theodora Endel, wife of ... Susannah Endel, wife of ... Ruth Endel, daughter of ... Rose Endel. I knelt to brush away the moss. That Rose Endel had died in 1781. Aged 24. 'It doesn't say why?'

I did not realize I had thought aloud until an 'I beg your pardon?' made me jump as if one of the graves had opened.

The tall, thin middle-aged lady in a tweed coat and silk headscarf smiled apologetically. 'I'm so sorry, my dear, did I startle you – but – oh no! This is ridiculous! You're so like him, you can't be anyone else! You must be Rose! Rosser's daughter!'

'Yes.' I smiled. 'You obviously knew my father!'

'Knew Rosser? My dear child, I can't remember the time when I didn't know your father and uncle. I'm Anne Wenden. I was Anne Gillon. That line over there belongs to me and those on the right are my husband's people. I've just left him playing the organ for Evensong at St Martin's – my brother's the vicar there and has his Evensong at three as if he waits till evening his church is so cold he doesn't get any congregation! As I took care of my eternal soul by going early this morning, I thought I'd come out here for a walk. It's such a perfect day, isn't it? What a pity June couldn't bring you to lunch yesterday. You knew I'd asked you? Never mind, you must come over to Shepland on your next visit. And how's June?'

We walked back to the church. She unlocked the door as I explained June's headache.

'Poor dear,' she clucked kindly. 'She has so many migraines. But let me look at you! Dear me! Seeing Rosser's daughter a grown young woman makes me feel every year of my age!'

I was delighted to have run into her. It was such a gloriously normal event and after the last couple of days, normality I needed. 'You were a great friend of my father's?'

She smiled. She must have been a very pretty girl. She was still fine-looking in a faded way. 'Rosser Endel was my first serious boy-friend. At the age of sixteen I was in love with him for one whole Christmas term. He took me to my first dance. He was then all of eighteen!' Her smile vanished. 'June told me about your husband. As we've just met, this may sound hypocritical, but as I knew Rosser so well and he was one of my dearest friends, I really am distressed for you. You're such a child.'

'Twenty-three, Mrs Wenden.'

'And the fact you think that's old shows just how young you are! You must marry again,' she said briskly, 'and before long. Don't leave anything too long in this life. That old truism about it always being later than one thinks is perfectly correct, even at your age! Shall we sit?' She opened the waist-high door to one of the high-backed and boxed-in pews. 'Walking now gives me a backache though as I love walking I refuse to give it up. It's rheumatism, of course. The curse of the marsh! And so poor June's unwell again? I am sorry. Of course, what that poor girl needs is a baby! I know it's none of my business and my children tell me I'm always sticking my nose into other peoples' affairs, but I do most sincerely wish I knew the present Endels as well as I knew the last generation. It's time someone gave them the advice they're crying out for. That huge house needs children! It is a tragedy poor June can't have any, but as she can't they should face up to it and think seriously of adopting.'

I was too startled for discretion. 'But she's having one – they hope. Oh Lor! I shouldn't have let that out! She wants to keep it a secret.'

Mrs Wenden raised manicured eyebrows. 'Has June told you she's pregnant?' I nodded and she looked perturbed. 'Dear me. What that poor girl obviously needs more than anything else is a good psychiatrist. Poor June – and poor Robert.'

I stared. 'I'm sorry, but I don't understand this.'

'So I perceive.' She straightened her skirt. 'You haven't been told June fell down the stairs at Endel when she'd only been a bride a few months and spent most of the last year of your grandfather's life, seeing gynaecologists?' I shook my head. 'I expect Robert doesn't care to talk about it. It must have been as much of a blow to him as it was to Old Robert. Endel had always gone to an Endel and because of the entail can't go to anyone but a born Endel. That's why you must marry again. If Robert dies childless, as he will unless he remarries and since adopted children can't be included, Endel will come to you.'

I was too astonished to grasp more than the odd detail. 'Endel's entailed?'

'Of course it is! Most old family houses are and that's how they stay in the family. You didn't know? Didn't you ask?'

'It never occurred to me to do so.'

She said, 'You may look an Endel, Rose, but you're far from a typical Endel if you can ignore the Endel estate. Did your mother never tell you?'

'No. I don't even know she knew. I can't ask her. She's dead.'

'As well?' She folded her neatly gloved hands. 'Poor child. I'm very sorry. I could weep for you. I did weep for your father when we heard he'd died at sea.' She looked at me with deepset brown eyes that looked backward. 'Dear Rosser. He was a sweet boy. I hope he found happiness in his short marriage.'

'My mother said they were very happy.'

'I'm glad.' She blinked. 'There's only one good thing in this present tragedy. If Robert dies childless, the Endel legend will die with him. It only applies to the men and can only be transmitted by the men.'

'You believe that legend, Mrs Wenden?'

'My child, I'm a marshwoman. I believe all our old legends. I think.' She smiled self-derisively. 'I was very relieved, if very surprised to hear Old Robert broke the threat, but if anyone could be termed a law unto himself, it was your late grandfather. I expect young Robert was secretly relieved. He's marsh – and according to my children, we're all a bit touched! Tell me, does he know June's told you she thinks she's pregnant?'

I hesitated. 'Yes,' was all I said.

'And he's not put you straight. I can understand that.'

'You can?' I asked eagerly. 'I can't.'

'You will, if you put yourself in his place. June's his wife and from all I've heard he is a most devoted husband. Between ourselves, though I'm sure June has great virtues, I've always been surprised he should choose such a plain little woman with so many pretty young girls around, but the world is full of ill-assorted couples and I only wish most were as happy as your cousins are reputed to be. Probably his being motherless from birth had a lot to do with it. He wanted a mother rather than a wife, but she is his wife, and being a good husband, he's not letting her down, even to a cousin. After all, though one look is enough to prove your blood, you are very much a stranger to Robert. Naturally he wouldn't want to expose his wife's weaknesses to a stranger.'

'So that's why.' I was not wholly convinced, because of my first night. Robert had not had to tell me to cover up anything June had said. Yet he had volunteered the information. As a safeguard? Probably. Yet he had looked so happy. 'Mrs Wenden, June couldn't by now have recovered from whatever she did to herself when she fell?'

She said simply, 'Rose, last spring, after seeing endless specialists, she had a hysterectomy. It was hushed up, but I heard, as everyone hears everything about each other on the marsh. We're all so inter-related. Our domestic helps are all related.'

'Not in Endel.' My words slipped out.

'I've heard there's been a general post up there since Old Robert died. Understandable. June's not a marsh-woman and we aren't the easiest of folk to get along with. I hope she's got some good women?'

'Oh, yes. Very good.'

Her eyes appraised me keenly. 'My dear, don't take this deception too hard. It's more tragic than anything else. And don't think this has never happened before. You may not have met it yet. You will, sooner or later. My father was a doctor. He had any number of patients who vowed they were pregnant when there was no possibility of their being so. I can remember one housemaid when I was a girl who went a bit off after she'd had her baby, insisted she hadn't had it, and even swoll up again! Then she produced all the symptoms of labour. Poor June. Poor any woman in her situation, but particularly poor June. Robert I'm sure will have treated her gently, but Old Robert!' She sighed. 'I'm afraid your grandfather considered the bearing of Endel heirs as the sole function of Endel wives. I wonder if they told him? For the peace of mind of all concerned, I hope they didn't.'

We sat in silence and the clamour of my thoughts deafened me. If June could twist one fact, what about the others?

Mrs Wenden stirred. 'You don't remember your father at all?'

'No. What was he like?' It was an odd question to have to ask a complete stranger. It was no odder than I felt. 'I'd like to know.'

She took her time. 'I'll be honest with you, Rose. Rosser was the only Endel I ever cared for. I was sorry Richard died, but he and I had never done more than tolerate each other. He never even asked me to meet his pathetic little French wife. The first time I saw young Robert, he was nine years old. Since when I've seen very little of him. I called on June as a bride. Your grandfather made it very clear he didn't welcome my presence in Endel. Old Robert had a long memory and he knew I'd been Rosser's childhood friend. I should have had the courage to ignore his displeasure for June's sake. I'm afraid she's made few local friends. I must see what I can do for her – and I'm determined to see more of you.'

'And Robert? He's really very nice.'

She said very politely, 'I'm sure he is, dear. I've never had the chance to know him, as I've explained. My own fault for allowing your grandfather to frighten me off. But then Old Robert frightened everyone – with the exception of your father. Rosser was the one person I've ever known who could stand up to his father.'

'Yet he left home?'

'Yes. He walked out and slammed the door. He wasn't thrown out.'

'Do you know why?' She didn't answer. 'I don't, nor does Robert. I'd like to know. Do you?'

She hedged. 'Why dig up the past which you and Robert have had the sense to forget? When all concerned are dead?'

I said, 'If only to stop me wondering if my father would be furious at my coming back.'

Mrs Wenden spoke as if choosing her words. 'Not furious, perhaps, though he was in a white fury when he left. He was very young and he had his share of the Endel temper.'

'You saw him before he left? After the row?' She nodded reluctantly. 'He must have told you what it was about as you were his great friend. Didn't he?'

'Yes.' She paused to make up her mind. I waited in the quiet that was over a thousand years old. She said, 'I'll tell you all I can remember, though whether this is fair to Robert and yourself, is something you'll have to decide. Just remember it happened a long time back. I was just back from Finishing School and your father home for

112

the Christmas vac. from Cambridge. Robert was a few weeks old. It was January 1939 and there was an accident on a marsh road in a night mist. Your father and the friend driving him, were in an open sports car. There was oil on the road. The car skidded into a dyke and overturned. They should both have been drowned, but as marshmen seldom drown in our dykes unless drunk, Rosser got himself and his friend's body out.'

I shuddered. 'Horrible – but why the row? You did say it was an accident?'

'Yes.' Suddenly her face was as blank as June's.

'Where exactly did it happen? Near Endel?'

'Just beyond the farm.'

'Why was there oil on the road? After rain?'

She hesitated visibly. 'The mist dampened everything. It hadn't rained that day. But a tractor had gone down the lane shortly before. It proved to have a leak.'

'An Endel tractor?' She nodded. 'Who drove it?'

'Richard Endel.'

'My father blamed him? And Grandfather sided with Richard? That it? Was it Richard's fault?'

She said, 'He was completely cleared by the inquest. There was the usual investigation. No one was legally to blame and it was generally agreed after that if anyone had been responsible it was young Dr Gairlie for driving too fast – and where's the young man, doctor or otherwise, who doesn't?'

'Yes.' That 'Gairlie' had struck a chord. I couldn't place it exactly but felt in some way it concerned, of all people, my mother. 'Who was this Dr Gairlie?'

'Old Dr Hethers' young assistant-cum-locum. The boy who was too late to deliver Robert and tried so hard to save Hélène Endel. Rosser had met him at Cambridge. I think Angus Gairlie then lived there, but may be wrong. He was a few years older than Rosser, but they got on very well. It was through Rosser that he came down to the marsh, which made everything so much worse for your father. He was nearly beside himself with bitterness and grief.'

'But it was an accident—' Her expression now made me catch my breath. 'It was an accident?'

'I've told you the legal verdict.'

'But my father didn't believe it?'

'No.'

'But – but – Mrs Wenden, if he was in the car – his own father and brother – they wouldn't want to kill him? Or that young doctor? Would they? Did they?' I urged, horrified. 'Did they?'

She said, 'My child, all I can keep repeating is the legal verdict which was not arrived at without proper investigation. Remember your father was a hot-headed, grief-stricken young man. And after remembering, forget it all. It was all over years ago. Your father arrived at my parents' house in the middle of the night after that row at Endel. He stayed the rest of the night and left the following morning.'

'And never came back.'

'He did. Once. A year later. He stayed with us and refused to go near Endel or contact his family in any way. He came down for a private memorial service here and had a plaque put up in memory of his friend. Come.' She stood up stiffly. 'I'll show you.'

The plaque was brass and fixed to the church wall between the list of local men killed in both wars and the list of those drowned while serving in the St Martin's lifeboat.

The plaque read: 'In memory of Angus George Gairlie, M.B., B.Ch., of Edinburgh, who was drowned in a Midstreet dyke at the age of 23 on the 11 January 1939.' Beneath was a smaller inscription: 'This plaque was erected by his friend Rosser Endel of London.'

Looking at the plaque I placed that chord. I had found a photograph of it in a desk drawer as a child. My mother had said, 'It belonged to Daddy. He must have wanted to keep it, so I've kept it.'

Another chord placed itself. '"To David Gairlie Loft-house on the occasion of his twentieth birthday from his Godfather and Uncle, Kenneth Gairlie."'

'Mrs Wenden, did Angus Gairlie have any family? Did they come to the inquest?'

'His father came for that. He was a Professor of some nature, then, I think, working in Cambridge. He died before the memorial service. Dr Gairlie's younger brother came down from Edinburgh. He stayed overnight with us.'

'Did he go to Endel?'

'No.'

'So he blamed the Endels too?'

She said quickly, 'I've no grounds for agreeing. He was a quiet young man. He said very little. He seemed grateful to your father. I forget his Christian name.'

'Kenneth?' I suggested.

She was startled. 'Yes! How did you guess that?'

I did not want to lie to her. I had to have time. I said, 'I remember now my mother showing me a photo of this plaque. She couldn't explain it and I'd forgotten it.'

'And I expect she mentioned Kenneth Gairlie. Perhaps she found the name in some of your father's letters. Extra-ordinary,' she said, 'the tricks memory can play.'

'Extraordinary,' I echoed.

CHAPTER TEN

The sun was touching the marsh and the birds in pairs were flying back to their nests. There were no lights on in Endel and it threw a sombre shadow. I heard the Monster as I opened the front door. I had to force myself to walk into the dim hall.

'Put on the lights, Rose,' called June sleepily from the sitting-room. 'I've been too lazy. Nice walk? You've been ages. Where'd you go?'

'Around Midstreet.'

I went up to my room and took down my suitcase from the top of the solid mid-Victorian wardrobe. I opened the case on my bed and then just looked at it for a couple of minutes before replacing it again on the wardrobe. I had done too much running away, mentally as well as physically. Sometime one had to stop running so why not now when there was only one more full day to get through?

Before I left, somehow I must talk privately with Robert. June needed psychiatric treatment nearly as much for his sake as her own. The strain of maintaining what he knew to be an act, must at times be intolerable. That would get worse not better. It could already be responsible for a great deal of the tension in Endel. That had increased since David moved in, but it had been there before.

Endel. A beautiful old house, but not now a happy house. Had it ever been? Or had some basic flaw in the Endel character made that as impossible in the past as it was in the present? Robert was covering up for June exactly as I had for Charles. How many other Endel men and women had tried to live a lie, tried to kid themselves kindness in that context was not synonymous with weakness?

Not that Robert looked weak. I contrasted his face mentally with my own in the mirror. His was the stronger and in repose, despite his fine-drawn features, surprisingly tough. Surprisingly? I thought of Grandfather's portrait. I turned from the mirror.

Should I tell Robert of David's almost certain connection with Angus Gairlie? That would entail repeating most, if not all, Mrs Wenden had said. It might split the family again. Yet if Robert and I saw much more of each other, the split was bound to come, if for another reason. And if David was sick enough to have killed Dolly and was Angus Gairlie's nephew, then his renting End Cottage was too sinister a coincidence to leave untold.

I had no chance to talk to Robert alone for the rest of that day. The men went down to the cottage to finish clearing there after they left the farm and returned with the news that David was standing us dinner in Astead. Robert drove us in the estate car. June fussed throughout the drive over the rising mist. 'We'll never get back!'

'We will,' Robert assured her. 'This is going to lift.'

'But, darling, I heard the forecast before we came out. They said no change.'

'They can say what they damn well like. This is going to lift and soon. I can smell a change. If not, I'd never have let us come out. A bad mist at this season means a sod of a bad one.'

The temperature dropped sharply during the dinner. There was no mist on our return drive and when we reached Midstreet the breeze was strong enough to make the rushes sing.

Murdo had come back and seen to the fires. David went up to the flat to pay Murdo the money he had won off him. He joined the rest of us in the sitting-room about twenty minutes later. 'No night-cap for me, thanks, Robert. Will you all mind if I go up? There are some letters I must write.'

'Make yourself at home,' said Robert, 'though I'm afraid you won't find the light in your room very good.'

'So I discovered last night.' David leant against the door, smiling lazily. 'I put 'em off. If I could do that again. I would, but the bloody things can't wait any longer. I wonder – could I borrow your sewing-room, June? Or do you just hate the sound of a typewriter, Rose?'

I shook my head. I didn't like the idea of him next door to my room, but this would get him out of the way. The Endels were exchanging glances. Robert said slowly, 'If Rose doesn't mind – help yourself.'

'Darling,' June squeaked in a whisper as the door closed, 'I know you hate people using your study, but was that wise? He'll be so near Rose.'

'If the noise doesn't bother her and she locks her door, I don't feel we have to worry. He's now realized I'm keeping one eye permanently on him and Rose has made it very clear that as far as she's concerned he's *persona non grata*.'

He gave us another drink, took his glass and sat on the arm of June's chair. 'If I may say so, Rose, you hand out the finest frozen mitt I've ever seen!'

June was not amused. 'I'm not joking!'

'I know, my sweet. You may be right – and you may equally well be wrong.'

'After Dolly?' she demanded.

Robert glanced at me, anxiously. As June had asked me to keep her confidence quiet, I said nothing. He said, 'Dolly's death has shaken us all, but I do feel we should keep the picture as clear as possible. Accidents do happen. Sometimes.'

June wasn't drunk, but she had drunk enough to forget caution. 'And sometimes they're caused intentionally!'

'Sometimes.' He stroked her hair. 'You know your trouble, darling? You're over-tired and over-het-up. Why don't you knock that one back and go on up. Rose'll understand. We'll finish our drinks and follow you in a few minutes.'

June stifled a yawn, swore she wasn't sleepy and had no intention of wasting this rare opportunity to have a cosy chat. 'If only David wasn't here! It's so nice. Just the three of us.'

'Rose'll be with us again – often – after he's gone. At least' – he smiled and I felt weak – 'we hope so.'

We talked for about an hour. They planned my future visits, the outings we'd take, the people we'd meet. They talked of June's baby. I watched Robert covertly as she said she hoped it was a boy.

He didn't flicker. 'I'd be as happy with a girl. I'm not fussy!'

I remembered Charles and how I had grown so into the habit of lying about him that there had been occasions when I had almost believed the lies myself. Only with Maria had I been able to relax. She had had to know the truth as she had been our only resident maid and cleaned our separate bedrooms.

Their conversation made an ideal opportunity for them to tell me about the entail. They didn't take it, possibly assuming I already knew. I could have mentioned it and explained briefly about meeting Mrs Wenden. I did neither. I still needed time to myself to think it over and that, in Endel House, was something that since my arrival I had only had at night.

June looked very tired and as she was as obviously determined not to leave me with Robert as he had been all day to take David off my back, I made the first move for bed.

June came with me as Robert wanted a word with Murdo. We heard David's typewriter in action from the stairs. June walked with me to my room.

'I hope he stops soon! That tapping would drive me crazy! You're sure it doesn't bother you?'

'Positive.' (For one thing, it fixed David in one spot.) 'You'd feel the same if you'd been married to a writer. Honestly. Charles worked mainly at night.'

'How – odd! Didn't you mind?'

I smiled politely. 'Got used to it. I even got to finding it soothing. In fact, there's no sound more calculated to rock me to sleep.'

She clearly did not believe me, though that was true. Charles writing had been a different and nearly happy man. It had been the periods when his typewriter was covered that I had learnt to dread.

June said good night. 'Don't forget to lock after me,' she hissed in a stage whisper.

Having locked, I sat in the armchair, using my foot to switch on the electric fire. It did not give much heat, but it took the chill out of the air, if not out of my thoughts. For once, these did not immediately concern myself. I thought about June. One day, someone, somewhere, was going to say something that would force her to accept the fact that she was barren. Robert couldn't continue to shield her from inquisitive friends and neighbours indefinitely. Without proper medical help, when that day came, June would crack. Surely Robert must realize that and that his kindness was misplaced? Or was he too close to her to appreciate how very close to the edge she already was?

I heard him coming up the stairs, switching off lights *en route*. He paused on the landing, I guessed, to listen. The typewriter next door was tapped spasmodically. It was the thought of David's acute hearing as much as June's reaction that prevented my going quickly out to ask Robert to fix some private ten minutes with me tomorrow. He walked on, his footsteps fading down the long corridor.

My room was warmer. Another five minutes and it would be warm enough to get undressed. I was in no hurry or mood for sleep. I sat on in my armchair long after those five minutes.

The wind was rising and though still no gale, already it trebled the usual nocturnal chorus of the beams and floorboards. It could turn into a gale when the tide came in and if the rain now falling kept on, the dykes would be full before the tide was at flood.

Angus George Gairlie, drowned in a Midstreet dyke.

Rosser Endel, not drowned.

Rosser Endel had believed his brother had tried to murder him. Why? I didn't know. Why not? Cain and Abel? My father had believed it sufficiently to leave Endel for good. Did it matter now? How could it? They were all dead. Forget 'em.

How? How many thousands of years since Cain slew Abel? Still remembered. I had to remember. I was Rosser's daughter. And Robert was Richard's son.

I'd had enough. I got up, restlessly, and went over to the wardrobe for my dressing-gown. The door opened before I reached it. David was sitting in the wardrobe. He swung his legs to the floor and stretched them. 'If you're always so reluctant to get into bed with yourself, love,' he

120

drawled, 'why don't you do something about it?'

My immediate reaction was neither surprise nor fear, which surprised me later when I thought about it. In the event I was too angry for thinking. 'What the hell do you think you're doing?' I realized I could still hear the typewriter. I jerked a thumb. 'What's that?'

'Tape-recorder.' He stood up and brushed himself down as if this was a normal social occasion. 'As I wanted to see you alone and knew I'd not have the chance unless your cousins thought me otherwise occupied, I got busy with the gadgets. I had to take the calculated risk no one'd bother to look round the door to check up. Neat, you'll admit?'

'One way of looking at it.' I managed to get my anger under control and to speak quietly, even gently. I needed no more to convince me he was unbalanced. Robert's room was too far for my loudest shout to reach him through closed doors and my door was locked. 'Why do you want to see me alone?'

'Oh, Christ! Are you really that dumb? Haven't you got the message yet?' He came closer. 'Do I have to spell it out?'

I stepped back a little. 'No. Not really. So you've had this long wait in that wardrobe for nothing.'

'Like hell I have! I had to sit it out in case lover-boy decided to pay you another nocturnal visit. How else could I've got you to myself, undisturbed?' He pulled off his glasses and deposited them on the tallboy. 'Let us not beat round the bloody bush, love! I've just got to get through to you if you're not going to turn into a stiff like Dolly!' He came still closer. 'Am I right in suspecting June's told you I bashed in her bloody brains?'

I backed again. I was now against the dressing-table and my mouth was very dry. 'June gets odd ideas. I – I don't pay much attention to them. Dolly was killed by a falling tile – like Robert said.'

'Oh, no.' Suddenly his voice softened. Suddenly, I was

121

terrified. 'It was no accident, Rose. I'm sorry to have to do this to you, but I can't see I've any alternative and—' His voice stopped abruptly as I hit him on the side of his head with a speed that surprised us both and all my strength. I hit him with the back of my solid silver-backed hairbrush which I had grabbed instinctively when his tone altered. In other circumstances the instant astonishment on his face would have amused me. Then he went down. He made hardly any noise as he fell limply. I gazed at him as appalled by my own violence as by his provoking it.

He was so still that for a hideous moment I thought I had killed him, then I saw he was breathing and breathed out. The cut on the large bump behind his right ear was bleeding on to his collar. The sight sickened me and the brush slipped out of my wet hand. I didn't pick it up. I walked round him, gingerly. He didn't stir. I turned my back to unlock the door and run for Robert – if my shaking legs would carry me.

I shouldn't have turned my back. I didn't hear him move, but I hadn't turned the key before his hand was clamped over my mouth. He lifted me away from the door holding my hands behind my back. His hold hurt.

'Stop fighting me,' he gasped, 'or you'll break one arm if not both! Hold still, damn you! Bitch!' I had bitten his hand, but he did not move it. 'I'm not hurting you for fun! I just want you to listen! Stop it!' He shook me. 'Lay off and listen! I didn't bash in Dolly's head. It wasn't bashed in. She died because she was poisoned – and check that with Murdo as it was he who told me. Don't ask me who gave her the stuff – your guess is as good as mine – but just remember poison is reputed to be one of the less attractive feminine weapons. And talking of females,' he continued breathlessly as I was still struggling, 'the ghost that gave you the screaming heebies yesterday wore a twin-set and pearls, and I saw her, though as I've no means of backing that up you probably won't believe me! Tell Robert that if you like and don't be surprised by his hurt

122

denial! Just remember, she is his wife – and though we saw his car returning – we didn't see the occupants! You didn't see your pal Bert driving me back, either, but as he just missed running over Dolly, he can tell you I didn't let her out! If you do check with Murdo,' he added more calmly, as I had stopped fighting, 'you might ask him whom he saw leaving my cottage yesterday morning. You don't have to believe him either, but you might try asking. I can't back him up as I was miles away, but as I wasn't alone any time you want that proved you can have it!' He lifted me up and dumped me on the bed. He breathed hard as he glared down at me. 'After slugging me like that, my girl, you're bloody lucky rape doesn't happen to be one of my hobbies! Slug me again and I'll slug you back – and don't think I wouldn't hit a woman!' He unlocked the door, chucked me the key, went out, then – incredibly – knocked before returning. 'My glasses, please.'

Shock turned me into a zombie. I got off the bed and handed them to him. 'Why did you take 'em off?'

'It's damp in that wardrobe, warmer here. Hot air rises. Soon as I stood up the change in temperature misted 'em up. Why'd you think?'

I had no answer.

He said drily, 'You're still not sure, are you? Even about that icicle.'

I shook my head.

'If it's any consolation, love, nor am I. Going to tell on me?'

'I can't think straight. God knows.'

'And worketh in mysterious ways.' He gave me a long calculating look, then quite casually reached out and ripped my dress from neck to waist. 'We all have our own ways of getting our kicks, Rosie. But murdering bitches just somehow leaves me cold. I'm funny that way. Good night.'

He closed the door quietly after him. The tapping stopped next door. I heard him leave the sewing-room and go along to the guest-room.

CHAPTER ELEVEN

June came in with my early tea looking as if she had also spent half the night up in a chair. She sat heavily on the side of my bed. 'David's gone.'

Some of my tea spilt over. I replaced the cup and saucer on the tray. 'To an hotel?'

'London. He's just left. He was too late to go with Murdo, so he's borrowed the mini. He's going to leave it in Astead station yard, collect his own car if it's ready, if not he's going up by train. He says he'll be back when End's habitable, but Robert doesn't think he will. He's taken everything he brought here yesterday – even his books. He left a message for you.'

'Oh? What?'

'Just goodbye and that he's sorry about last night, though he doesn't expect you to believe him.' She waited expectantly then had to ask, 'What happened last night?'

I couldn't tell her the truth so I kept it brief. 'He made a pass and I clouted him.'

She was half annoyed, half amused. I could see her angle. 'So that's how he got that cut behind his ear. He said he'd slipped.' She giggled. 'Slipped up!'

'Quite.'

'But how? I mean – I heard you lock your door. Why did you let him in?'

I glanced at the wardrobe and lied calmly, 'I hadn't got undressed when he knocked so openly I thought it must be you or Robert.'

'Then he pushed his way in?'

'Sort of.'

She patted my hand. 'My dear! I'm not surprised you didn't want to talk about it. He didn't – hurt you?'

'Not in the way you mean. He made me bloody mad.'

'Oh my word! I'll bet you!' She flapped her eyelashes. 'Robert's so clever! He guessed it was something like this! He said David looked so sneaky just now that he obviously didn't dare face you and would be the same about us after we'd heard your story. He'll be as sorry about this as I am, though we're not sorry to see the back of that man! When Robert came to bed last night he said he was fed to the back teeth with the way he's kept pestering you. He now wants him out of End as much as I do. So now we don't have to worry about him any more!'

I made no comment. She made the mistake people often make with women and took my silence for acquiescence.

The wind had dropped, but it was still raining hard at breakfast. Robert said nothing about David until June went into the kitchen to discuss meals with Mrs Hodges. He got up to close the door. 'I know what you told June. I want now the bits you left out. Just what did that sod do to you?'

I might have told him the whole truth had his expression been less similar to Grandfather's in that portrait. I stuck to facts. 'We had a sharp hand-to-hand struggle. He got clouted with my hairbrush and my dress got torn to the waist.'

He flushed dully. 'Why didn't you scream?'

'Because most of the time his hand was over my mouth. Oh yes – I bit his hand.'

That had an odd effect. Very briefly a flame of triumph flared in his eyes. Then they were only concerned again. 'That got rid of him?'

I just nodded and watched him as closely as he was watching me. It was rather like seeing him for the first time. I saw his attractions and suddenly, how well he used them. As now. 'I could throttle him.' His voice shook. 'But, to you? My dear, what can I say? How can I begin to apologize for exposing you to such an unpleasant experience under my own roof?"

'It wasn't your fault!'

'Rose, dear, of course it was! It's not as if June hasn't

125

warned me! I could kick myself from here to ruddy King-
dom Come for the way I've ignored her. But as I've always
assumed that overdose of radiation must've sterilized him,
I thought he had to be harmless as any gelding. I wrote off
all June's talk of his being sex-mad as just another example
of the way-out notions a woman gets when she's pregnant.'

I did not want to trap him. I had to try. 'If she wasn't
pregnant, you'd have believed her?'

'I would, indeed!' Again his voice shook with sincerity.
'Rose, you won't let this spoil Endel for you?'

It was my turn to lie. 'Of course not, Robert!'

'You don't know how much it means to me to hear you
say that.'

He was dead right. I didn't.

A queer and almost peaceful sense of detachment in-
vaded me. June came back and I seemed to watch us all as
if I were a ghost in David's empty chair. I heard them make
all the right sympathetic remarks and myself the right
answers. I had always thought June a phoney. Now there
seemed nothing between her and Robert and myself.

I turned my new eyes on David mentally. I had originally
disliked and distrusted him simply because he reminded
me of Charles. Had any girl slugged Charles in similar
circumstances to last night, he wouldn't have raped her but
would probably have killed her. It was owing to his temper
being uncontrollable that as his wife I had learnt to control
mine. In that wild moment of fear last night, I had forgotten
that. And suffered only a few bruises on my wrists and a
torn dress in consequence. But my dress hadn't been torn in
anger. Then why had he torn it? I looked at Robert. Though
the Endels wanted David out, had he worked on it all
month he couldn't have come up with a better reason for
not daring to face me again this morning. And were he
genuinely as sick as they kept insisting now and June
previously, would he have been capable of the self-control
he had shown towards me?

I scrapped the idea of that talk with Robert. The man

126

I wanted to get alone was Murdo. I was still wondering how, at lunch, as June had shadowed me all morning, when Robert asked if I'd do him a big favour?

'Of course, if I can?'

He smiled the smile that yesterday had made me weak. Yesterday was a long time ago possibly as last night had been a very long night.

He asked me to drive into Astead with Murdo and the helps in the estate car and bring back the mini. 'I can't leave the farm today, June shouldn't drive with that wrist and it's hellish inconvenient having only one car. The mini keys should be in the booking office, but I'll let you have the spare in case the sod went off with them. Murdo'll see you into the mini. Take it easy out of Astead. It can be pretty busy around five when the market closes. I want Murdo to do a couple of jobs in Astead, but they shouldn't take long. He'll probably overtake you before you're on the marsh and lead you back. I'll brief him. You'll do that?'

'With pleasure.'

They beamed on me. 'Isn't she sweet?' squarked June.

'Very,' said Robert.

The rain had stopped. The sun broke through after lunch, the clouds moved out to sea and it was warm enough for spring. Later, when Murdo drove us down the cinder road the marsh looked more beautiful than I had yet seen it. The grass was more green than yellow, the tips of the rushes were pale orange, the sky was pink and gold, the air very still and the sea a distant murmur.

Murdo sniffed the air. 'There'll maybe be a mist.'

The helps in the back said they wouldn't be surprised, neither, if the wind didn't get up late same as it done last night. I had not previously exchanged a word with Mrs Hodges, and Mrs Smith seldom opened her mouth in Endel, but they both now chatted non-stop like children let out of school. They discussed the drunken brawls that had followed the match, Mrs Franklin's holiday-camp weekend, the bad luck that nice Mr Lofthouse was having with his

127

cottage and did I know he was a Dr Lofthouse and ever so clever even if he wasn't a proper doctor as you might say They sighed in unison over Dolly's death. 'Give me a real turn to see her old basket empty in the boot-room this morning,' said Mrs Hodges. 'I mean, a dog gets to be like one of the family, don't she? Mind you, like Mrs Endel says, she'd a good long life and she were getting too stout for her own good – but you can't help missing her.'

Murdo was silent. The ladies eyed his back sympathetically. 'Taken it real hard,' they mouthed to me.

We dropped Mrs Hodges on the outskirts of Astead, Mrs Smith in Station Road, then drove on over the railway bridge and into the yard. Murdo got out. 'Yon's the wee mini. I've to collect a parcel for Mr Endel. I'll away to the office for the keys, ma'am.'

'Thanks. I'll come with you as I'd like to stretch my legs before driving back.' I looked up at the now crimson and amber sky. 'Glorious evening.'

'Aye. Maybe.'

'You don't think it'll last?'

'If it does there'll be a shocking wee mist this night. It's too warm. But it could change in no time at all. That's often the way of it on the marsh.'

He enquired for the parcel while I collected the keys and returned to me frowning impatiently. 'It's not in yet! They say it'll maybe on the next down train. I'd to say I'd be back. Mr Endel'll not thank me if I return without it. It's a wee giftie he's ordered special for Mrs Endel's birthday in the morn.'

'Tomorrow? I'm glad you told me. I didn't know. Are the shops still open?'

'Aye. Till six. As I've to go up the town, can I be getting anything for you?'

I hesitated. I would have preferred to do my own choosing, but if there was a chance of a mist, I did not want to delay too much. I had to talk to him, which might not be easy on a shopping trip. 'Could you get me some flowers and a card?' I gave him a pound. 'This do?'

'Aye. What flowers would you wish?'

'You'll know more about what's available now than I do, so may I leave that to you? And could you keep the flowers in your flat until tomorrow?'

'I'll do that.'

'Murdo,' I said, 'this is very kind of you. I say, I've had an idea. How long have you to wait?'

'Forty minutes?'

'Then have we time for a quick cup of tea in the buffet before we go our separate ways? I feel just like a cup – and perhaps you can then tell me exactly which road to take back in case I have to do most of the return on my own?'

His deep-set little eyes studied me warily. 'Did Mr Endel not provide you with a wee map?'

'No. I expect he forgot.'

'Och, aye. You'll mind we'll be needing platform tickets to get into the buffet?'

I sighed inwardly in relief. 'I'll get 'em.'

The station buffet was newly decorated in mock-teak and scarlet. The waitresses wore pale blue nylon overalls and served tea in paper cups. It was good tea.

We sat at an empty table under the clock. I gave myself ten minutes. A longer delay would have to be explained. A quick cuppa could be forgotten. As I could not afford to waste time, I didn't. I told him how upset I was for him as well as myself over Dolly's death and how upset she had been when I came off that tractor on Saturday. 'I didn't learn till later that she'd seen a man killed off a tractor in that same field when she was a puppy.'

He had been listening woodenly. He sat forward. 'And how was that? Since there's been no fatal accident in Endel farm for over twenty years as old Mr Endel told me many a time when he'd to take to his bed and I was in his room to give him a wee hand when he'd a wish to use the toilet and was too heavy for Mrs Endel.'

129

I stared momentarily. 'He said that? He couldn't have been confused after his stroke?'

'Aye, he was that, times. Not about this. Farming can be a terrible dangerous profession, and there's a wee marsh committee set up to advise the marsh farmers on the prevention of farm accidents. When any marsh farm has had no fatal accident for twenty years, they hand out a fine certificate to the effect. They came to hand Mr Endel his when he was on his sickbed. He showed it me.' He smiled slightly. 'Och, he was that proud of it!'

'I see.' I only wished I did. 'I must have got this wrong. Not that it makes any difference to how sweet Dolly was. I liked her so much – and you loved her. She adored you. You must have had an awful shock when Mr Endel broke the news.'

His wrinkled gnome's face twisted. 'I'll not deny I'd a great affection for the poor wee doggie. She was a grand lassie.' He shook his head. 'She'd formed an affection for yourself, ma'am, and for all her douce ways she'd not do that to all.'

'I'd noticed that. She seemed very fond of Mr Lofthouse,' I added slowly.

'Aye.'

'He seemed fond of her.'

'He was that.'

'Bad luck about his boiler, wasn't it?'

'Aye.'

I glanced at the clock. Five minutes gone and he was wooden again. 'It can't have been easy for Mr Endel to tell you. He didn't enjoy telling me she'd been killed by that falling tile.'

'It wasn'a from Mr Endel I heard!' He looked as if the words had burst out and as he couldn't take them back had to go on. 'It was the birds.'

'Birds?'

'Och, the wee geese!' He actually winced. 'When I went back of the stables to feed them on my return – you were

130

all away out, you'll ken – they were away down the field scrabbling some new turned earth. I fetched a lantern – and had to away for a spade. She'd not been lain deep enough.' He grimaced. 'It was a sad spectacle. I'd a great affection for that old doggie,' he added pathetically, 'and I'm no' ashamed to admit I was greeting like a lassie when I finished the job.'

'Murdo, I didn't know. I'm terribly sorry. I really am.'

'I ken that well.' He met my eyes with rare steadiness for him. His eyes were wet. 'I'm an awful daftie about animals. It's my weakness.'

'Mine, too.' I hated to press him. I had to. 'And Mr Lofthouse's – I think?'

'That's a fact.'

Was it? I had to be sure. 'Murdo, I'm going to ask you something which you won't want to discuss and I won't enjoy. But I must know. How was she killed?'

He shifted his gaze. 'I'm no' a veterinary surgeon, ma'am.'

'I know, but, if there'd been marks on her body, her head, wouldn't you have seen?'

'Maybe.'

'Were there any?'

He took a long time before shaking his head.

My chest felt tight. 'Would you know how a dog that had been poisoned would look?'

'Maybe.'

'Was that how she looked?'

He shuffled nervously in his chair. He knew he'd already said too much. He wanted to say more, but he didn't know if he could trust me. I was Robert's stranger cousin. Robert gave him work and a home. Though he had two trades, he was too old to get another job easily. But Dolly had liked me and had probably been the one creature in years to have loved him. He had no visible family ties and at sight looked a shifty, scruffy little grafter. Dolly hadn't minded. She settled his indecision now.

'You'll mind this is just for your ears, ma'am?' I nodded.

131

'To my way of thinking she'd been put away with a wee drop of poison.'

I caught my breath sharply. 'Mr Lofthouse said that.'

'Aye. I told him.'

I shook my head, but that didn't clear my thoughts. 'Murdo, how? Surely, she was too wise to touch anything poisoned?'

'Och, she'd not touch a poisoned bird on the marsh and many's the one she'd pass by after the one wee sniff, but she'd a terrible weakness for a sweetie. She'd take anything in a sweetie,' he added with grim misery, 'anything at all!'

'I didn't know that. Murdo, is there any poison in Endel?'

'There's aye the stuff on farms. For the rats, you'll ken. There's aye a few rats in the cellars up the house. The stuff Mr Endel uses now to keep 'em down'll not harm domestic animals, but there's many a jar of the old stuff they used when he was a wee laddie down the cellars.'

'What kind of stuff?'

'Och, I'm no' a chemist, ma'am!'

'No. I'm sorry.' My mind was building up a new, frightening, but still blurred picture. 'Murdo, who gave it to her?'

He went grey with anger. 'It's no' my place to put words to the thoughts I've maybe in my head!' His 'r's' vibrated with suppressed fury. 'But I'd be asking for my cards and away to the Exchange before I'd work one day for any man that to my way of thinking had put away old Dolly. She was my friend! I'd have ye ken, ma'am, I'm a MacDonald not a bloody Campbell! I'd best be drawing you that wee map!'

'Yes. Please. Thank you.'

He used the back of an old envelope. His drawing was clear, his handwriting as he put in the road names and landmarks, was extraordinarily educated. 'If you keep to that, you'll not get lost.'

'Thanks.' He was on his feet, but I hadn't finished. 'Naturally, I'll not upset Mr Endel with any of this.'

'Is that a fact?'

132

'Yes. Though it obviously won't be news to him.'

'Och, no.'

'I imagine he used that falling tile story to spare' – I hesitated – 'people's feelings.'

He said bleakly, 'I've no doubt you're right.'

June, I thought, June. I'd been so busy peering under stones, I'd forgotten to look at the stones themselves. 'Murdo, one last thing.' I explained Dolly's behaviour outside End Cottage on Saturday morning. 'I forgot to tell Mr Endel. Do you think I should in case it was a stray tramp?'

'That'll not be necessary.'

I swallowed and managed to sound casual. 'Was Mr Endel in there that morning?'

'Och, away, is he not the landlord? He's a right to see to his own property in his tenant's absence.' He jammed on his greasy cap. 'If I'm not away I'll miss the shops.'

I apologized for keeping him and thanked him. 'See you on the road back, I expect.'

'If that wee parcel comes in on the next down train. If not, I'd best wait on. Mr Endel's that set on having it this night.'

'He said that?'

'Aye.'

I didn't have to believe him. I just did.

I had another look at the clock as he shambled off. It had only taken fifteen minutes, so it should still be twilight when I got back. The Endels would be waiting for me and we'd be all alone in Endel. 'How cosy,' June would say.

I wondered what she had said to Dolly when she offered her that sweet.

I left the buffet, handed in my platform ticket, went out into the station yard. The colour of the clear sky had altered again. It was now all yellow and the white mini had a yellowish tinge. I got in, and started the engine for only one reason. I didn't know what else to do.

CHAPTER TWELVE

The light began to blur on the new highway. In Coxden, the bare chestnut trees lining the wide main street looked feathery, the old houses seemed smaller and the grey church with the tall square tower had muzzy edges.

It was a relief to have an excuse to drive slowly. The longer I delayed, the less time I'd have in Endel before Murdo got back.

I was too confused, too sickened and too much of a coward to work out precisely why I now so dreaded the prospect of Endel and the Endels without some outsider to dilute the strain, but not to make up my mind on another point. Tomorrow, the Endel family history was going to repeat itself, if not so dramatically as previously. I would write them a bread-and-butter letter.

The lorry directly ahead of the mini slowed abruptly as the road narrowed between the overhanging houses, crawled through the narrow and on to the single-track stone bridge over the Marsh Ditch. I waited until it was off the bridge to drive on and as it turned into the marsh road, a man stepped from the shelter of the bridge wall and directly in front of the mini. It was David. I had either to stand on the brake or run him down.

He wore a dark city suit. His white shirt had thin black stripes and the tips of the pointed collar were buttoned down. His tie was dark blue silk. He looked uncharacteristically and incongruously urbane against the wide flat backdrop of the marsh. I gave every trivial detail of his appearance the acute attention I always gave trivialities in moments of emotional shock. It was a form of self-defence.

He opened the passenger door and got in. 'As I'm still in one piece, I presume you've checked with Murdo?'

I was back in my zombie-routine and nodded dumbly.

He glanced back. 'Get moving, Rose. You're causing a jam.'

I drove off the bridge, waved on the cars behind, then pulled up at the Ditch side of the road. The water was like a mirror and two swans were admiring their upturned reflections. 'Why aren't you in London?'

'Changed my mind.'

'Why?'

He lit a cigarette. 'For one thing, I forgot to ask your vital statistics. I don't want to buy the wrong size when I replace that dress.'

'You're going to do that?'

'Yes.'

'That's why you were waiting for me here?'

'Yes.'

'How did you know I'd be along?'

'Our Murdo. He rang me in Astead two hours ago.'

'Why?'

'Because I paid him five quid to keep in touch.'

I smiled without humour. 'How much did you pay him to spin me that tale about Dolly?'

'You talked to him. If you think he was lying, work that one out for yourself.' He paused. 'Was he lying?'

'How the hell do I know now?' I snapped. 'How can I know anything about anyone connected with Endel? Including you!'

'How the hell do you expect to know anything?' he retorted impatiently. 'While you insist on letting your emotions cloud every issue? You've got a brain, Rose! Try using the bloody thing for a change.' He was silent for a few seconds. 'Well? Was he lying?'

'Perhaps not, though I'd not put it beyond him to sell out on his grandmother for a fiver.'

'His grandmother, maybe, but not on an old bitch over whom he's wept the first tears he's probably shed in forty years. This is Britain, love. We British may overlook some-one taking a swipe at our wives and kids, but God help

135

anyone who takes a swipe at our dumb friends – even if we do need an RSPCC on the job as well. June probably can't appreciate just how Dolly's death has got Murdo under the belt. Robert, of course, has. No fool, our Robert.'

'June can't appreciate – because of her allergy?'

'Not merely that. She spent most of her formative years first in Sweden, then after a short interval, Australia. Her stepfather's Australian. Didn't she tell you?'

'Only that her mother'd remarried. You sure? She doesn't talk like an Australian.'

'They don't all talk 'Strine. She does, occasionally. Oh my word, I'll bet you, she does!' He mimicked June's squeak cruelly well. 'Haven't you noticed? Or her clobber? Those dead-beat twin-sets? Would you be seen dead in 'em?'

'No. Her clothes have puzzled me. I just thought she'd no fashion sense.' Vaguely I recalled Adrian. 'But she said she's lived years in England.'

'Just over three. She met and married Robert within months of arriving in London. Endel's a long way from the King's Road, Chelsea.'

'Yes. Why,' I thought aloud, 'tell me wrong?'

'Either to impress you, or mislead you. Take your pick.'

I looked at him curiously. It wasn't just the suit. He was sounding as unlike his previous self as he looked. 'David, just what's going on? Is anything going on?'

'We could go back and ask them.'

'You can't come to Endel! Robert'll throw you out!'

'So you showed him that dress?'

'Just told him. Why? You wanted me to?'

'Sure. I'm an exhibitionist. Haven't you rumbled?'

'No. No!'

'You may, yet. Let's move on. Robert may be out for my blood, but he can't chuck me out of my cottage without a court order which he knows I know he's unlikely to get.'

'You can't go back there! It's got no water or heat!'

'I'll survive – I hope,' he added rather grimly. 'And if

you don't get a move on, at the rate this mist is rising, you won't be driving anywhere, with or without me. What do you say? Taking me along for the ride?'

'Do I have any choice?'

'Sure. You can carry on alone and risk being stuck out alone all night, or if you beat the mist you can get back to the jolly party they'll have all laid on for your last night. What'll you do, I wonder? Sit round knocking back the wine and chatting over by-gone Endel days – hold it, I forgot! You and Robert look forward, not back! Dead wise! When the past has so many murky moments.'

'Don't all old families have 'em?'

'Don't ask me. The farthest I can go back is to a great-great-grandfather who was a miner and fathered eight kids before he died of the dust at thirty-one. My age. Not that I wouldn't like being able to trace back the way you Endels can to – who is it? Adam? Noah? No.' He snapped his fingers. 'Those two lads – Cain and Abel. Or did they crop up quite a while later?'

'Just what is that supposed to mean?' I asked and made up my mind. If he lied now, I'd turn the car round, drive into Coxden and ask for the nearest cop's house. If that didn't get him out of the car I'd say he was molesting me – anything. Robert would certainly back me up and Robert was a local landowner and employer of local labour.

David said, 'This may not mean anything to you. But once I had an uncle called Angus Gairlie.' He raised his eyebrows. 'I see you know it! How long have you known?'

'Not long.'

'Have you told Robert?'

'No.'

He didn't ask, why not. He didn't say anything. His expression was taut and his eyes were guarded. We watched each other in silence, then I switched on the engine and checked in the driving mirror. It looked safe to move off, so I did. I hoped it was safe.

The world had gone sepia. The marsh, the dykes, the

rushes, the sky, were all sepia. The colour had that eerie quality of the colour in dreams, or advanced French films. I observed it, absently.

David said, 'I'm sorry about your dress, though it didn't suit you. You shouldn't wear blue. Didn't your husband tell you?'

'Yes.'

'That figures.'

We were silent again.

A low translucent cloud had risen over the marsh. It had been stationary and only a few inches high. Then it developed a gentle swell and rolled over grass and dykes and lapped the edges of the built-up roads. Each time the miniature billows rose higher than they fell.

I said, 'The ghost of the lost sea returning.'

'Uh-huh. And the tide's coming in. Shall I drive?'

'No, thanks. You don't have to be nervous. I've driven in London smogs.'

'Sure I've to be nervous! A London smog's a piece of cake compared to what this may turn out to be. Still, if you're driving it will leave me free to keep an eye out for trouble.'

'Expecting trouble?'

'Anyone who doesn't on this marsh in a mist needs his head examined. Had your IQ tested?'

'Not since I took the eleven-plus. Why? Have you?'

'Many a time, specifically since that natty little gadget worked itself up and blew myself and a couple less fortunate through a roof not so long ago. Shall I tell you something mildly interesting?'

'Do.' I was tense.

'Strangely, perhaps to you, though it didn't do me a lot of good, it didn't bugger up my IQ, and I've the medical reports to prove it. Show them to you, sometime. They're so impressive I'm thinking of framing them.'

'Psychiatrists' wonder boy?'

'That's me! Spill the lad's brains out of his ears and he

still comes up with the right answers. Though it could have been that they just happened to ask the right questions.' I felt him watching me. 'Did the Endels warn you I'm a right nut?'

'They told me about your accident.'

'Plus trimmings? Yes?'

'Roughly.'

'Roughly! From the way you looked at me last night, you'd me lined up as stark raving bonkers! Which reminds me, love, that you need some advice. If ever again you find yourself in a locked room with a man you think that, for Christ's sake lay off the violence or you'll get yourself into a headline in the Sunday newspapers. Didn't you realize that?'

I said, 'Yes. Later.'

He said thoughtfully, 'Which is why you bothered to check with Murdo and stopped just now?'

'Yes.'

'I hoped it would do the trick.'

I glanced at him. 'You've worked it all out?'

'It didn't work out exactly as I'd intended. I didn't expect to come out of it with a God-awful headache. But after Murdo told me about Dolly when I went up to pay the bet I owed him I thought it time someone forced some questions into your head, and as I told you last night, knew I'd not a hope in hell of getting you alone, if I didn't creep up on you. So I fixed my tape-recorder and got into your wardrobe. Simple.'

'Was it? How did you manage to get that tape ready so fast?'

'Didn't take any time. That tape was mostly a play-back. It runs five minutes, rewinds, runs again.'

'Clever.'

'Brilliant,' he drawled. 'I had to set a time-switch and push all of three buttons. Hey – watch it!' I had swerved the car badly. 'I don't know about you, but I've no urge at all to end up like dear old Uncle Angus and dear old Dad and getting out of a mini underwater'll be a bloody sight more tricky than getting out from under an open sports job. How did you hear about that?'

'I met someone who knew.'

'When?'

'Yesterday afternoon.'

'How did you connect me?'

I told him about that flyleaf and the plaque in St Mary's Midstreet. I didn't know if that was wise. He had seen the plaque. He asked now why I hadn't told Robert.

'No time, yesterday.'

'And today?'

I said, 'I changed my mind.'

'How about me?' he asked softly. 'How about me? The late Charles D. still in the way?'

I sighed. 'I'm sorry. I know it's not your fault.'

'Don't apologize, love. Your antipathy's the best compliment you can pay me.'

'How so?'

'Think. Think of the men in your life to date. Think of those you've loved. Think I'd want to be lined up with that little bunch of perverts?'

I grimaced as if he'd hit me and didn't answer.

He went on, 'I looked up a man I knew at Cambridge on Friday. He's produced some very good television documentaries. He can't help being queer as they come. I thought he might have known something about your late. He did.' He paused. 'Shall I go on?'

'No.'

'Then let us discuss something else. Like the Endel family failing for picking the wrong marriage partner. Robert's a bright lad, and how he could have looked twice at June without recognizing her as a man-eater has beaten me since I first met her.'

'But she eats out of his hand.'

'And what normal man wants to spend the rest of his life feeding bits of himself to a woman with his own hand?'

140

The mist was over the road and half-way up the mini wheels. Round the next turning it was a thick white cloud on the road. I stopped. 'I can't see anything.'

He got out to look round. He came to my window. 'We can't stop here. The right dyke's just a foot from your front off-side wheel. Get her in low gear and I'll guide you over.' He reached for the steering-wheel. His hand covered mine. 'Don't be so bloody neurotic!' he snapped as I jerked my hand away. 'I'm not using this as an excuse to man-handle you. When I want to do that I don't waste time with excuses. Get her moving, or if anything heavy comes too fast towards us, we'll be strawberry jam. That's it. Steady on course.'

He walked some way with one hand on the car. In the next clear patch, he got back in. Then he was out again.

The drive that should have taken about forty minutes spun out into hours. The soaking white blanket became a soaking black blanket. It seeped into the car every time he opened his door to check the grass verge and was in our hair, our eyes, our chests. Occasionally, when he had to check by the light of the dipped heads, his head and shoulders looked as if he had been in a cloudburst. Directly he moved from the lights and groped his way back in he was invisible. The car had no internal lights and the one over the speedometer didn't work. He struck a match to check the mileage. 'We should be near Midstreet Wall. Stop, Rose.' He opened his door. 'Yes. I hear the sea.'

I pushed open my window. 'I can't.'

'With Big Ears Lofthouse along, why worry?'

I said, 'I'll say this, without Big Ears I'd never have got this far.'

'Now, that,' he said, 'is typical of your muddled thinking. Without me to hold you up, you wouldn't have waited at Coxden, or even delayed talking to Murdo. Right?'

'Yes, but—'

'Belt up, and listen, Rose. We had about twenty minutes before it really clamped in on us. Alone and minus those delays, I'd say you'd very likely have got just about here before it got too thick and dark. We're on the sea-road now, so even alone you'd know all you've to do is keep on to the cinder road. Wouldn't you carry on? Alone? Having got this far?'

'Probably. At a crawl. Or I'd get out and walk.'

'And face our June without her precious mini?'

'I'd forgotten that point. No. I'd have tried to get it back to Endel.'

'Even after Dolly?'

I said flatly, 'As I'm far from sure she's responsible for her own actions, yes.'

'I'll go along with that.' He struck another match. 'I wonder in which pub Murdo's sitting this out?'

'Probably the station buffet as the bar'll be open, even if Robert's parcel has arrived.'

'What parcel's that?'

I explained. 'You know, it's June's birthday tomorrow?'

'Is it, indeed?' His tone was odd. 'Well, well, well — careful, woman! Don't crack the bloody wall from this side!'

'Sorry.' I had to back as the high cement wall loomed a couple of feet ahead. 'This is the worst, yet.'

'Want me to get out again?'

'Either that or you take over?'

'You may as well stay put. You get out and you'll probably walk into a dyke. This is my best suit and I don't fancy a swim.'

I waited until he got in. 'David, why are you really along with me? Just a boy scout at heart?'

He laughed. 'Perish the bloody thought!'

'Then — why?'

'Let's get back to Endel and then maybe you'll be able to answer that for yourself.'

'How?'

'Christ, woman! If I'd a crystal ball, how could I use it in this black-out?'

142

'I wish you weren't so damned evasive!'

'Huh! Look who's talking!'

'David, this could be serious—'

'And if you don't keep your eyes on what little you can see of that road ahead you may make history by for once being right! The dykes round here are the deepest on the marsh and the notion of ending up as yet another plaque on the wall of Midstreet church does not appeal to me!'

'Sorry.' I slowed. 'Can I ask something else?'

'You can try.'

'Had your being Angus Gairlie's nephew anything to do with your originally coming down here?'

'Indirectly, yes. I knew he'd died down here, though no one in my family had mentioned it in years up to the time I saw the advertisement. I came down, I quite liked End, but the marsh I liked – and like – very much. I like the space, the wind, the sea. I miss my industrial grime, and yet this marsh is for me. I wrote to my mother to ask if she'd any objections. She is still not exactly sold on things Endel, but said that as all concerned in her brother's accident were dead, as I liked the place, that was enough for her. She didn't ask me to sound local views on the old subject, but having time on my hands I've done that while handing out the odd beer, mainly because I like working on problems.'

'Can I ask what results you've had on this one?'

'Sure. None.'

'What do you mean?'

'That, as I've already told you, your grandfather is remembered as a bloody-minded old bastard and his eldest son, incidentally, as a weak womanizer. I've had the impression no one would have put Old Robert past murder, but as he'd no call to bump off a singularly harmless young locum whose name no one even remembers, plus his youngest son, it must have been, as the inquest verdict said, an unfortunate accident. You may be interested to know that the only thing that still surprises the older locals about

143

your father's walk-out is why it didn't happen earlier, since he and his old man were always at each other's throats.'

'Is that so?'

'So they say.'

'You believe 'em?'

'Having, as you know, a nasty suspicious mind, I tend to regard unproven facts as unproven.'

'Is that why you never told Robert your mother was a Gairlie?'

He said, 'This you mayn't believe, but originally I kept it quiet as I don't generally like digging up old dirt. Then you showed up at Endel, all was sweetness and light – despite the Monster's merry pranks – and I didn't want to spoil the party – until it began to get somewhat out of hand – hold it!' He opened his door. 'Coming up to the cinder road any moment now. Hard left. Ready?'

'Yes.' I could hear the murmur of the sea. 'The tide sounds way out.'

'It won't be. It's coming in. Steady as you are. Almost there.'

I couldn't postpone the thought of our arrival any longer. 'What happens when we reach Endel?'

'Let's get there, first. Left – now! Easy! This cinder isn't as slippery as macadam, but this isn't built-up as high as the main roads. There's a small dyke on our left and a dirty great main dyke on our right.'

'I haven't forgotten.'

'Good,' he said, 'as after all the rain last night and this morning both'll be full – watch it! Hard left! I can hear an engine revving!'

I heard it then and almost simultaneously the oncoming headlights broke the mist. They were much higher than the mini's lights and absolutely blinding.

'Keep your foot off the brake, Rose!' David wrenched the wheel round to the left to take us on to the few feet of grass between the road and the smaller dyke which we knew to be there even if we could not see it. As something large roared by the mini did a complete circle, then shot crab-like across the road and straight into the main dyke. The headlights went out immediately the bonnet hit the water. The little car rocked once, then began to sink.

In the pitch blackness, David grabbed my arms. 'No! Don't try and get a door open yet!'

'Are you really out of your mind?' I fought him, uselessly. 'We must get out! We're going down!'

'That's where we'll stay if we don't use our heads! We can't open a door until the pressure in here roughly equals that outside. We try it and the water'll come in too fast and she'll go down like a stone, plus us!'

We were sinking more quickly. The water was round my chest. It was so cold, so dark and the remaining air was so foul with the acrid mixture of dyke, petrol, oil and carbon monoxide. Already, lack of oxygen had us both gasping. 'Sorry – and to have landed you in this—' My voice was jerky because of the poisoned air. I was too shocked for fear or hope. 'My fault.'

'It's not – and it's no accident.' He hauled us both up in our seats and pulled my head back to catch the last air trapped under the roof. 'If you make it' – he gasped painfully – 'and I don't – tell the cops – check Somerset House – this is attempted murder – now!' He covered my mouth and nose with his hand and managed to get his door open. As he kicked us both free the mini dived downwards.

CHAPTER THIRTEEN

I thought we would shoot upwards. Instead, I felt myself being dragged backwards under the water for what seemed like a lifetime. My head was bursting and my hunger for air was so primitive that could I have kicked myself free and got up alone, I would have done so. Then we surfaced and a reed whipped my face. After the icy slime below, the black night air was warm as a caress.

David held my head above water and supported my body against his as we gulped in mist. 'All right?'

'Yes. Thanks.'

'Easy,' he muttered, 'just take it easy.'

I was too exhausted to do anything else. I rested my face against his and was conscious of the expanding and contracting of his chest and, at first, very little more. I didn't know if he was treading water or standing. I could feel nothing but tangling reeds beneath my feet. As I caught up on lost oxygen I grew dimly aware we were surrounded by high rushes, mist and silence. I forgot the cold, the wetness, all David had said in the car, or that I had ever done anything in my life but gasp for air.

'Rose.' David's lips touched my ear.

'They're coming back. Don't move or talk. Get me?'

I remembered then. Fear was far colder than the dyke water. David wasn't taking any chances. He held my mouth shut with one hand, hitched one leg round both mine and had me in such a grip that I could not move at all. I had no desire to move. I was too tired and suddenly too frightened. David had known how to handle the situation in the car. I hoped he still did.

I heard the footsteps his keener hearing had already caught. They were muffled by the mist, coming nearer and belonged to more than one person. They stopped somewhere close to us.

'That mini must have over ten foot of water above it by now.' It was Robert's voice and it travelled like a whisper. Despite David's warning I might have called out but for his hand. 'As it sounded as if it suddenly dived, she probably got a door open. That'll have finished her.'

June's squeak carried more clearly. 'I didn't hear that. I couldn't see anything, even before the lights went out! I'm glad! I couldn't bear to see my lovely little mini in all that dirty water! I wish it'd been the estate car! I love my mini!'

'It'll clean off once it's dry, Junie. Don't fuss!'

'Honestly, darling? I so hate dirt!'

'Yep,' grunted Robert. 'Good as new. Unlike my charming cousin.'

'Robert, I'm so glad!' June was enthusiastic.

Robert said drily, 'That makes two of us, my love. You didn't hear anyone shouting, either?'

'Should I have?'

'I trust not, but had she got out she'd naturally have yelled for help and one of us must've heard her. She's down there, either in the mini or stuck in the reeds and mud as her body hasn't come up and there's no sign of her at the grating. If she's in the reeds the tide'll take her out under the grating by morning. Hush! This may be your brother, but it could be Murdo. Who's that?' Robert shouted and the mist carried his shout back as an echo.

'Rob? You there?' The reply floated softly.

'On the right and round the back of End! Watch your step, mate! I've done enough dyke fishing for one night. Still no sign of her at the grating?'

'None that I could see.' The new voice was close enough to be recognizable. Incomprehensible though it seemed, I recognized it as Adrian's. 'What now, Rob?'

'The tractor stays down by the wall until daylight or this lifts. As the mini must now be jammed in sludge and there's not a hope in hell anyone inside could still be alive, no one in his senses 'ld be expected to risk dredging till he can see what he's doing. Try it, and it wouldn't be the first time a rescuer plus rescue-vehicle's gone the same way as the victim. The fact that we've managed to get a tractor this far plus lifting tackle is just further evidence of our good faith.'

'Isn't Robert clever?' squeaked June.

'I'll hand it to you Rob. God! My dears,' said Adrian, 'this is a damn sight colder than the Tyrol! My knee's playing up after all the hanging around.'

'What we all need is a drink,' said Robert. 'Anyone say no?'

June said, 'I wonder what David'll say?'

'After his invaluable lapse last night,' retorted Robert, 'sweet fanny adams, unless he wants to talk his way out of a rape charge. One word out of him and I'll tell plenty to the cops, including my personal theory that it wasn't only the weather that made her skid by End. I'm – of course, un-happily – convinced she either thought she saw a ghost – or, if necessary, the bloke that mussed her up last night. Either'd be enough to set her off without the weather as a bonus. In any case, I'm going to tell 'em to check with David that she was capable of working herself into hys-teria over non-existent ghosts in Endel and when the lights failed, even though she should've learnt from her first even-ing that my machine's packing up is a routine Endel event.'

Adrian said, 'I'd like to have heard you on the haunting job, Rob.'

'He sounded so spooky at night, Adrian – and I made a wonderful ghost when I took over on Saturday! Oh my word, I did! It was Robert's idea! He thought it all up that day you rang from Innsbruck to say you'd met her on the way out.'

'Not all, then. Just the rough outline. Mostly I played it by ear. Come on,' said Robert, 'one more look and we'll have that drink.'

A speck of light glowed faintly. Silently we slid under water. Their footsteps were fading when we surfaced and I was shaking violently.

'Relax,' muttered David. 'All over, *pro tem.*'

My teeth were chattering too much for me to explain I was not shaking with fear or even cold. After so long in the water I was too numbed to notice the temperature. I was shaking with anger, a large part of which was directed at myself. I had never known such fury. It rose in waves and each wave pumped more adrenalin into my bloodstream.

When we eventually groped and floundered up the slip-pery bank and flopped like stranded fishes on the path round End, I was almost warm. David was shivering as uncontrollably as I had in the water.

He sat up. 'I've some whisky inside. Stay here. I'll get it then get you in.'

'No.' I stood up unsteadily, but on my two feet. I had lost both shoes. I didn't remember when. 'I'll manage. But can you?'

'Just about.' He was on his feet. He dropped a soaking arm round my soaking shoulders. 'Like I said – tough cookies, you Endels!'

I was too angry and he was too cold for involved explanations, but he had saved my life, so the least I could do was save his ego. 'I've the biological advantage of more subcutaneous fat. Let's get in.'

The back door was unlocked. The kitchen was the only room in the cottage that faced Endel. There was an oil lamp and matches on the kitchen table, but we did without light until we had had some neat whisky and fixed a blanket over the low window. The lamp gave a gentle orange light and the faint smell of paraffin was sweet and clean in comparison with the smell of ourselves.

We were caked with black slime, oil, strung with broken reeds and dripping dyke water. My jersey suit had been coral. No one would guess.

David had lost his jacket, tie, shoes and one sock. His striped shirt was ripped across the chest, his trousers were clamped to his legs and his bare foot was filthy. He said, 'The clothes are wrong, but otherwise you look exactly like a primitive woman after her first climb out of the primeval swamp.'

'That's how I feel. I'm sorry about your best suit.'

'Too bad, isn't it? Let's clean up.' He enlarged the rent and pulled off his shirt and string vest. His chest was crisscrossed with puckered scars that stood out pinkly against his fair skin even under the film of slime. He saw me looking at them. 'Six months off on full pay.'

'They hurt?'

'Not now.' The slime on his face was drying. The patches

149

he had rubbed clear round his eyes and mouth made him look like a badly made-up Black and White minstrel. His eyes were very bloodshot and blinking furiously.

'Have you got any spare glasses here?'

'Not sure. Maybe, upstairs. I'll see when we've got this muck off. I've towels here.' He opened a cupboard and took a pile. 'The tank's empty, but the pump's working. It'll be cold. Ever had a bath in a kitchen sink before?'

'No.'

'I'll scrub your back, then you can scrub mine.' He swung the pump handle. It clanked and gurgled for a few seconds before the water came out in gushes. Pumping with one hand, he rinsed his head and shoulders. As the water was cold and soap useless, he used washing-up detergent powder to shift the oil.

My long hair was revoltingly matted. It took ages to get even tolerably clean. I re-tightened the towel I was using as a sarong and rubbed in more detergent. 'Sorry about this.'

'It has its compensations even without my glasses. Ready for the next lot?'

When we finished washing the stone floor was flooded with dirty water, the kitchen was icily damp and the living-room without its boiler and with the gaping chimney, nearly as bad. We used his bedroom, covering the low window with the flock bed-quilt as we were using the remaining blankets on ourselves.

David carried up three old-fashioned oil heaters, stood them in a row and lit them. 'I'll shove a kettle on one and we can have some tea. Be milkless. Mind?'

'Frightfully. I'm not stopping.'

He had found his spare glasses. He looked up at me over his shoulder as he crouched by the heaters. In the soft light his face was as taut and his eyes were as guarded as when we drove away from Coxden. His expression contradicted the lightness of his tone. 'Ask me nicely and you can have it laced with Scotch.'

'I'll do that.' I hugged my blanket. 'You wouldn't have

150

any clothes here?'

'I don't think – no, wait! Out of the road!' He dived under the bed and produced a suitcase. 'I'd forgotten this one! It's not even unpacked.' He opened the case. It was filled with ski clothes. 'This is where we came in.' He helped himself to a selection. 'There's more than enough for the two of us. You get clobbered up. I'll put on a kettle and have a check all round below.'

'Aren't you going to dress first?'

'Downstairs. I'm shy.' He smiled slightly. 'Nothing like a good Non-Conformist upbringing for inhibitions.'

'David, wait.' Belatedly I noticed the phone. 'Shouldn't we use that?'

'It's dead. I tried it when I came up for my glasses.'

'They even fixed this one?'

'Obviously. No gale. No swans fly in mists. And had you got out you might just have made it in here alone.'

'Huh! They weren't taking any chances!'

'Does that still surprise you?' He went downstairs before I could answer.

I put on a cotton T-shirt, long sweater, nylon underpants, ski trousers and ski socks. After the damp draughty blanket, the warmth and comfort of clothes was inexpressible. My damp hair was still uncomfortable, so I stuck it on top of my head in the yellow tea-cosy hat he had worn when I first saw him. I was looking at my reflection in the bureau mirror and looking back, when he returned with a tray loaded with teapot, kettle, cups, a tea-caddy and the whisky bottle. He was wearing the black roll-neck sweater and black ski pants he had worn that first day. The quilted anorak with the mandarin collar was still in the suitcase.

He pulled it out after depositing the tray. 'Shove this on, Rose.' He chucked it at me. 'You need it.'

'No, thanks. I'm warm enough.' I handed it back. 'You have it.'

'I'm not fighting this one out.' He left the anorak on the bed and got busy with the kettle. He poured two whiskies

151

into the cups. 'Keep us going while that thing boils.' He sat on the bed. 'Come and sit down.'

One side of the bed was against the wall. We used the wall as a back-rest. Ever since we had got out of the dyke, intentionally I had been suspending thought. I guessed he'd done the same. We couldn't do that any longer.

I drank my whisky at a gulp. 'David, why does Robert want me dead? I can understand June – even Adrian.' I shuddered. 'Did you know he was her brother?'

'Half-brother. Yes. I knew.'

'In Austria?'

'No. I'll explain that in a minute. You tell me first, why you can understand about them and not Robert?'

'Because of the entail at Endel, of course! As June can't have kids that'll end with Robert, if I'm out of the way. Wives generally outlive their husbands, and though she's older than he is, she's not that much older. Without me, she'll get Endel and probably hand it on to Adrian.'

He put down his empty cup, folded his arms and sat sideways to watch me. 'I didn't realize you knew about the entail, or that June can't have kids.'

'I heard yesterday.' I now told him all of that conversation with Mrs Wenden. 'She tried to hide it, but I think she still believes my father was right and that Grandfather and Richard wanted him dead. You do, don't you?'

'Yes.'

'That why, ever since I arrived here, you've kept rubbing in the past?' He nodded. 'You knew there'd be a repeat?'

'I didn't know,' he said. 'I just suspected, at first vaguely, and by Saturday evening, far from vaguely.'

'What made you suspicious? Adrian? Or your mother?'

'Both, though I was good and curious long before Junior came into the picture. I knew my mother's views on that old accident had to be biased. Until I took my first proper look round Endel and the estate, as the world's stiff with men who've walked out on their families, wives, kids, I wrote your father off as just another with an urge to get away from it all. But Endel is no suburban semi-detached, and to even a city lad like myself the marsh is fascinating. I've observed marshmen acknowledge no other form of scenic beauty. And from the way the locals and Robert talk, the Endels have always regarded Endel as the centre of the universe. Your old man,' he went on thoughtfully, 'had to have been brain-washed into thinking that way before he left the nursery. Yet he chose out – but once out, hung on to his surname and gave his only child an Endel family Christian name. Complicated character, your old man, and yet apparently uncharacteristically single-minded when it came to keeping away from Endel. He not only kept away himself. I don't know what he told your mother, but it was obviously enough to make her respect his wishes long after his death, even though, on the face of it, that should have been enough excuse for a young widow to seek a reunion with her husband's family.'

'It never crossed her mind – far as I know.'

'And you took it for granted, as kids do. Coming in from the outside, it struck me as dead fishy. People get over family rows – unless the basics are involved. So I got to wondering. Woman? Money? Hate? Or, the strongest of the lot, self-preservation? As the first two didn't seem to apply, it was a toss-up between the last two, if not a combination of both. If a combination, maybe my mother's views weren't all that biased. So last October I went up to Edinburgh to see Kenneth Gairlie, Angus' younger brother. He'd been a theological student when his brother died. He's now a Minister of the Kirk. I told the Endels I was staying in London.'

'Last October? You distrusted them then?'

'Wasn't so much that, though I never took much of a shine to them. Like I've said, I didn't want to stir up old mud, even if I didn't object to doing that as a private academic exercise. Old Kenneth gave me some good food and damn-all else! Which made me curiouser and curiouser.'

The kettle was boiling. He made the tea and remained standing. 'Kenneth Gairlie is a direct descendant by inclination, if not birth, of John Knox. He wears his principles in public. When I asked straight out if he agreed with the legal verdict, he refused to discuss the matter. Had he agreed, he'd have said so. I had to leave it in the air and come back writing it all off as another of life's unanswerable little problems. Until,' he said, 'until I had a letter from Murdo in Austria telling me there was a great to-do in Endel as the young master's long lost cousin had been found and hopes were high that she could be persuaded to spend a few days in the old homestead.'

'Murdo wrote you? Why?'

'Because I'd previously asked him to send on my mail from here. He shoved the lot in a large envelope and generally added a note. Despite his uncouth appearance, Murdo writes good English.'

I said absently, 'His handwriting's remarkably good.'

'Not remarkably for a Scotsman. He may only have had an elementary Scottish education, but as the Scots have always taken education seriously, he's far more educated than the average Englishman of his age and background. He enjoys writing letters and there's very little goes on in Endel that he doesn't hear as he pussy-foots round with his log-baskets. Not that that's hard with June's voice. It'd travel through ten feet of cement and then crack a man's eardrums! And June's often lonely. The lonely have to talk and June'll always prefer to talk to a man – any man – including Murdo. Murdo, also lonely, likes to talk. He's talked to me. I like him. I wouldn't trust him with my wallet or my whisky, but I'd trust him with my life.'

'Does he know you're half a Scot?'

'No.'

'Why haven't you told him?'

'For the reason I originally gave you in the car and also because the only way to keep anything quiet is to keep it quiet.'

'Yes.' I was trying to sort all this out. It wasn't easy, but I was trying. 'Did his letter tell you exactly where I was staying in Austria? He'd heard all that?'

'He saw your name and address on the envelope Robert gave him to post in Astead. He was posting mail to me that same day. He wasted a stamp opening the letter to add that bit. He put the stamp on the bill he gave me when I got back. So, being a curious bastard, I came on over, officially, to ski the Alterberg. And here's where what may be the only genuine coincidence in this whole affair comes in. I didn't fix running into you in that chair-lift queue. I wanted a couple of runs before turning up at your hotel and the lunch-break seemed the best time. When I saw you standing in front of me, I wasn't at all sure you were you, until you pushed up your glasses to check your change before buying your tickets. Even with your hair hidden, like now, your face and eyes are stamped Endel. So when I noticed the screw was loose in your boot-clip, I took it out.'

'That was you! I thought it fell out on the lift! Why'd you take it out?'

'To bring you down as it did. I hoped that'd provide more time for a respectable pick-up. I thought then it had loosened itself accidentally and in which case it wouldn't be a bad idea to have your skis looked over by an expert.'

'That's what my ski Lehrer said. David – it wasn't accidental?' He didn't answer. 'Adrian? And that icicle? Adrian?'

He shrugged. 'I can't prove that screw. And any good lawyer would make it hellish hard for me to stick that icicle on him. Personally, I've no doubts he was responsible for that little ploy.'

'Why?'

'His face had been bothering me all the time he was soft-talking you into accepting Robert's invitation. I didn't get the why, until he'd gone in to take that phone call and after I'd heard him talking as if he'd never heard of Endel till you had that letter.' He refilled our teacups. 'He came down here to visit June one Monday a week or so after I first moved in here. I knew it was a Monday as Robert was at Astead market. I remembered seeing him walk by my front room below that morning and then back and hitching a lift on the sea-road before Robert got back. I remembered thinking that if my landlord's wife chose to entertain lads in her husband's absence it was no bloody business of mine, and forgetting all about it. But that morning on the terrace, suddenly he made me dead curious. When I got out into the hall, he was going upstairs. So I asked old Skullhead at the desk if I could go up and take pictures. For fifty Austrian shillings he said Thirty and Thirty-one were empty and I could help myself. I went into Thirty. There'd been no sign of Junior on the stairs and he was very quiet next door, but I heard someone in there. I saw that icicle fall before I got to Thirties' balcony. I had to look over to see if you were in one piece and as you were, ducked back. I wasn't quick enough. I heard someone leaving Thirty-one. I didn't see who it was. I did see Junior on the stairs looking out of a window a short way down. He didn't look round. It was a good view, but from his colour and the sweat on the back of his neck, he wanted to throw up at the sight. Him and me, both.'

'Didn't you say anything?'

'Like, what? You'll never be a good murderer till you perfect your aim, lad? Or, better luck, next time?'

I shook my head, helplessly.

He went on, 'I knew I'd to be back in London next day. My firm had a special board-meeting lined up, they wanted me there and as they've been bloody good to me I had to show up. But I didn't fancy the notion of leaving you with Junior about to join your ski-class. Skiing's a dodgy enough hobby without one's would-be murderer in one's class. So I thought I'd fix that one. I chatted up a waitress, got his room number and got busy in the ski-rack during lunch.'

'You weakened his strap? You could've killed him!'

'Not very likely, as he was a good skier about to join a

156

junior class. It's always the top-class skiers in the top classes who do themselves the most damage on the slopes. I thought, at the worst, he'd bust a leg and hung around to find out. You know what happened. I knew, though I couldn't prove, what might've happened. Not pretty, love.'

'No.' I grimaced. 'Why didn't he wait for Robert?'

'Possibly because it seemed too good an opportunity to waste. Possibly because you're too damned attractive, his sister is not, and he was afraid that after meeting you Robert might weaken. He looked a bright lad, if not bright enough to guard against his own conceit. Had he been less sure of himself, he'd have checked his skis more thoroughly. He didn't, did he?'

'No. Luggi said that the next day.'

'Luggi—?'

'Our ski Lehrer.'

He nodded in silence.

I asked, 'Why didn't you give me a hint? Why let me go on thinking you were German until Herr Schneller put me right? The hotel porter.'

'Skullhead. H'mm. Why? You know perfectly well. You wouldn't have believed me. You wouldn't even have listened.'

'No,' I said, 'no. I wouldn't. I liked him. I thought him such a sweet boy.'

'And you didn't like being reminded of the late Charles.'

'No.'

'Figures, doesn't it?'

'That, yes. Particularly as you didn't then know he was related to June. When did you find that out?'

'Somerset House last Friday.'

'Why didn't you tell me?'

'And have you run straight to Robert with the glad news?'

'Yes,' I said bleakly, 'yes. I'd have done that. But, yesterday you wanted to talk to me—'

'As I told you last night, to try and force you into asking

157

yourself a few questions. Even then, I'd to be dead careful as quite possibly, most, if not all I said, would get back to Robert and make him wait until I was right away before showing his hand. I don't believe he's yet rumbled just how much I know. I don't think for one moment he wanted me permanently out of the way. He's well aware that if I run into a fatal accident a hell of a lot of people who specialize in the job of asking awkward questions'll be right on his doorstep doing their job. B.C.C.'s a good firm and like all good firms, looks after its own.' He grinned sardonically. 'Though it suited Robert's book in one way to have me walk in on Saturday evening, in another, it can't have done his blood-pressure any good. He fixed my boiler to blow, but not to take me with it, and previously I've always rung up before leaving London to ask Murdo to get it going to give me hot water on my return. So our Robert had to have me to supper. And as the Endels aren't in the habit of inviting me to evening meals, I thought I'd accept. Not having seen Murdo then, I didn't know he'd been in here that day.'

I told him about Dolly. 'I should've guessed it had to be Robert. I didn't. I guess, as I didn't want to.'

'Even Homer sometimes nods. Don't kick yourself too hard, as June probably said to Robert! I'll bet he wasn't consoled. He'd wanted me temporarily out of his hair, instead he'd me as a house-guest – the last thing he wanted!'

'But if he doesn't know you've rumbled him—'

'He doesn't have to, to want me out. From the start' – he tapped his chest – 'I've been far too interested in you. That he couldn't risk, so he went to work. I don't know what exactly they told you about me, but I do know that all that's ailed you hasn't only been my resemblance to the late Charles. It's really only since we got out of the water that you've looked at me as if there's a faint chance I'm a rational human and won't spring at sight. Right?'

'Yes, but that doesn't explain why Robert minded your interest in me, or why he wants me dead?'

He said, 'Turn that round. What's he got to lose if you live and either start asking questions yourself, or remarry some man who isn't an egocentric expatriate, who wants a wife for more than therapeutic purposes, and makes with the questions on your behalf?'

'What questions?'

'Like, the terms of your grandfather's Will. You do know what he left in hard cash?'

'No. Should I?'

'Of course. The Will was published.'

'I never read 'em.'

'Christ, Rose! You are a fool! Listen. After duty, the old man left two hundred and eleven thousand quid. Plus Endel, the farm, the live and dead stock, the land. Some of the money maybe he could share out as he liked. Not the Endel estate, as it's entailed.'

'I know that, but—'

'Just listen, woman! You know the entail applies only to legitimate kids of Endels?'

'Of course. Robert and I are the last two.'

'Correction, Rose. There's only one left. The daughter of Rosser Endel's legal marriage to Angela Mary Yeo, of King's Abbot, Devonshire. Rosser's elder brother Richard had a son by one Hélène Dubois of Paris, France, but he didn't bother to marry the girl. With me, now?'

CHAPTER FOURTEEN

He knelt to trim the wicks. 'I expect your chum Bert ran Junior out.'

I sipped the whisky he had just given me. It didn't make me feel less stunned. 'Openly as that?'

'Sure. He's part of the family. Naturally, they'd want him to meet Robert's long lost coz on the last day of her visit and if he did just happen to turn up after you'd left with

159

Murdo, once you were dead, who'd be around to suspect his timing wasn't purely accidental?'

'Did you guess he'd come down?'

'No.'

'But you guessed they'd try something tonight?'

'It seemed a reasonable assumption. I'd gone. Remove Murdo and they'd have you and Endel to themselves. Robert doesn't take unnecessary risks, but nor does he waste good opportunities.'

'Had you any idea how they'd try it?'

'When I saw what the weather was doing and added to it your being asked to bring back the mini, I'd a vague hunch. Robert'll have known this mist was coming and unlikely to lift. When you told me Murdo was waiting for that parcel, I was fairly certain my hunch was right. June's birthday's in July.'

'David! Why didn't you warn me in the car?'

'My hunch could've been wrong.'

I glanced at his carefully expressionless face. 'And even then you couldn't be sure I wouldn't tell Robert?'

'Precisely. He'd then postpone matters as he had to when that tractor didn't kill you on Saturday. As I've said, he doesn't take unnecessary risks.'

'But hasn't he taken one involving June and Adrian?'

'On the contrary. It was an accident – but – if the question of murder ever arises, as accessories to murder are as guilty in law as the murderer, it's all three necks or none. So no one can later blackmail anyone. Crafty.'

'Very.' I swallowed. 'And so are you and not only crafty. You risked your neck coming along for the ride.'

'Did I have any alternative?'

There was something I had to say, so I said it, 'No. You didn't. But were you really like Charles, nothing would have persuaded you to risk your own skin. He couldn't have helped running out on me. He was like that. Then, later, he'd have wept for us both. Genuinely.' He was watching me in a sombre silence. 'I made a mistake, but so did he. It

160

was hell for him, too.'

'Poor bastard,' he said, 'I expect it was.'

For a little while, neither of us said anything else. I broke the silence. 'Did you tear my dress to make sure I told Robert about last night?'

'Yes. And, I hoped, to make you yourself wonder why I'd stopped there.'

'I did.' I told him my thoughts on the subject and in Endel today. 'After that, then Murdo's talk, suddenly I was dead scared.'

He said, 'You got the message.'

I said, 'And my life. Thanks to you.' He said nothing. 'You get June's birthday from Somerset House?'

'No. She wasn't born in the U.K. She let out the month one night sometime before Christmas. They'd asked me in for a drink, she'd had a few gins, Robert was called up to the farm to see a sick animal and June was at the talkative stage. That's how I knew she'd a brother somewhere, and had chosen to stay at school in Australia when her step-father's job took him, her mother and kid brother back to Europe. She didn't mention names. I got them from Somerset House.'

He had checked the births, marriages and deaths of the last three Endel generations. June's maiden name, Ostlund, had been on her wedding certificate. 'In 1943, a widow, Dorothy June Ostlund, neé Evans married one Thomas Alan Browne of Sydney, Australia, in London. A son of that marriage was born a year later in London. Adrian Alan Browne. But there wasn't any record of any marriage between Richard Endel and Hélène Dubois. Robert's birth certificate is there.'

'There wouldn't be any record in England! They married in Paris.' He was shaking his head. 'You can't be sure!'

'Don't be such a bloody moron, Rose! Would I stick my neck out if I wasn't?'

'You've checked in Paris?'

'I've had a good solicitor checking for me. His firm have

French contacts. The French are dead keen on keeping their books straight. That marriage was supposed to have taken place in 1938, before the war could mess things up. There's no record of it anywhere in France. There never has been, but no one's been bothered by the missing evidence as until these last few days no one's bothered to look for it. Possibly your father would have done that, had he known the whole truth, but even then as there was still his father and Richard between the entail and himself, the war hadn't started, and it must've seemed highly probable Richard would remarry and have more kids, my guess is, he wouldn't have given a damn for his own chances. From his subsequent behaviour, he was too bloody sickened by his family to want any more to do with them.' He sat on the edge of the bed. 'If he did suspect the truth and later, after you were born wanted to do something about it, the war tied his hands. Then he died before Richard. As he can't have told your mother, as her subsequent behaviour proves, his death must have been quite a break for his father and brother.'

'Yes,' I said flatly, 'it must. But, if he didn't guess, why did they try and kill him?'

'Possibly because he asked enough awkward questions to get them really worried. If Angus Gairlie told him a quarter of the story he confided to his brother Kenneth on what was the last New Year's Eve of his life, your father'll have asked those questions and, in consequence, wrote Angus' death warrant and very nearly his own.'

'How do you know?'

'Kenneth Gairlie.'

'You said he wouldn't open up!'

'Nor would he, last October. I flew up to Edinburgh again last Saturday morning. You cracked his principles. Until then, he hadn't known you existed. After he was Ordained, he went into the Army and spent most of his war in a Japanese prison camp. On his return he was ill for about five years. He heard your father was dead, but hadn't heard he'd married. When I told him I thought your life was in danger but had no possible means of proving my statement, it did the trick. Poor old boy,' he said kindly, 'he'll be in a hairshirt for life after divulging what he regards as a cross between a professional confidence and a penitent's confession. He said I could tell you, but no one else without his written consent. He'll give it. Wrrrong, he said, must be rrrighted.'

'Angus knew? From Hélène?'

'Yes.' His face hardened. 'He thought he'd intentionally been called too late. She told him she'd felt ill all day and been asking for a doctor. After her death the Endels denied this flatly and reminded him his delay had been caused by the mist. She was dead. The mist was there. He couldn't prove anything. She'd told him she'd asked for a priest. Another flat denial. And Richard, who spoke fluent French, reminded Angus he didn't – which was true. Imagine what a good lawyer could've made of that in a witness-box.'

'But he could've proved they weren't married! And what about her family? Friends?'

'She was as devoid of close relatives as yourself. Her parents died in the First War. She'd been raised by a spinster great-aunt who died a few weeks after she started at the Sorbonne. The poor kid was only nineteen. She'd come to England expecting to marry before her baby was born. Admittedly, the birth was premature. Maybe Richard meant to marry her. Fact is, he didn't. She died in a strange country in which she'd had no time to make friends and didn't even speak the language properly.' He rested his face against the wall to look at me. 'This is your country. How many of the friends you must have scattered round England would query tonight's accident? Particularly after reading the verdict the inquest would've had to produce, had you been alone?'

'None.'

He said, 'As the locals say, chip off the old block, our Robert.'

He was silent so long, I'd to prompt him. 'Go on.'

He blinked. 'Yes. You said Angus could've proved Hélène wasn't married. Yes. He could. Had he been willing to break a professional confidence, to spread mud on a dead girl, to bastardise a harmless infant and blacken his great friend's family name. Yet, to keep quiet, might one day jeopardise his friend's future right to Endel. Poor devil, his Calvinistic conscience must have given him hell. He had to confide in someone, he chose Kenneth whom he knew he could trust. He told him the lot and said he'd just given your father a wee hint to put him on his guard. He didn't specify on what. It could be coincidence that a few weeks later he was drowned in a Midstreet dyke.'

'Kenneth doesn't think so, either?'

'He uses the Scottish verdict. Not proven.' He took a long breath. 'Had I not been along tonight, tomorrow, I'd have had to settle for that. I could pin the bastard label on Robert. Not your murder.'

'Would you've done that?'

'God knows.' He took off his glasses to rub his still very sore eyes. 'I'd have to have done something, and not just for you.' He closed his eyes. 'Junior's German should come in handy in South America.'

'He's going there?'

'If he's got any sense, he'll get there fast, change his name, dye his hair, and take his half-sister with him, if he values her life. Personally, I'd pick the upper reaches of the Amazon. The mosquitoes and the headhunters might miss. Like to bet on our Robert?'

'David! He won't try again!'

'Rose, grow up!' He snapped wearily. 'If, as he now thinks, he's got rid of you – if, as he might so easily have done, he got away with it once, obviously, he'll try again. June's got to go. He'll want kids. Can you see her ever letting him go?'

'No,' I said, 'no.'

'And as her death might just upset her dear little brother, if I were Robert, I'd have Junior next on the list. I wouldn't

164

wait too long, either and nor would I take any long walks with him along lonely cliffff-tops.'

'You think Adrian might kill Robert?' My voice cracked. 'Both?'

'As Adrian'll have even more to gain, he'll be a fool if the thought doesn't cross his mind after tonight. Nothing succeeds like success and they say murder's like adultery. The first may stick in the throat but after that it's a habit. And Junior has such a gay, impetuous nature.' He got up to deal again with the wicks and stayed standing. 'If it ever comes to the crunch, my money's on Robert every time. He uses his head before as well as during the opportunity. I may be wrong, but I've the impression he's already working on the right climate for June's unhappy accident. Possibly, suicide?'

'How? And what do you mean by climate?'

'How? Dead easy with anyone who takes as many sedatives and tranquillisers as she does. Or haven't you heard they don't mix with alcohol?'

'Yes. Yes. But, climate?'

'Has he told you, in strict confidence, of course, that she's pregnant? Or having a pseudo-pregnancy?'

'Pregnant.'

'That figures, in your case, as you might've heard about the entail and being a stranger could be kept well away from local gossip – he thought. As I'm known to get around the marsh, I had a straight man-to-man chat on her hysterectomy and the tragic misconceptions from which she's now suffering as a follow-on.' He smiled grimly. 'Stuck in the groove. I'm a nut-case, you're a hysterical neurotic, and poor June's a victim of the instant menopause – and we all know what that can do to a woman, don't we – and if we don't we've got our Robert to tell us. To make sure we all get the message, poor old Dolly was buried in too shallow a grave in a field in which the geese were bound to find her.'

'That was on purpose? To show she wasn't killed by a

tile? To make Murdo suspect June – as he does?'

'I think so.'

'It was June, wasn't it?'

He said simply, 'I thought so at first. Now, I'm not so sure. June would've used poison, but could she've got over her genuine fear of dogs to get close enough to Dolly to give it her? If she could, how about her allergy? I've known her sneeze for an hour after being touched by Dolly. That's why she'd to let Dolly out of Endel before going into her ghost act on Saturday. Dolly sensed you were in trouble and without anyone to hold her off, she'd have got in through the swing door. That would instantly have made June sneeze and put paid to that lark. Were you awake Saturday night when that door was banging?'

'Yes. I heard someone go down and then Robert's voice calling Dolly.' I shuddered. 'David, not then?'

He shrugged. 'Officially, that's when he found her dead. If that was true, someone must've been down earlier. I hadn't slept up to then. I didn't hear a step, a sneeze, a sniffle. Did you?'

'No. But yesterday at breakfast June's face was so puffy. Couldn't that be the after-effect of an allergic attack?'

'Possibly. Or she could've been weeping. She often has crying-jags. She may be a cold-blooded bitch about you, but she wanted kids. She knows she's failed Robert on that count and whatever else is her fault, that one isn't.' He looked me over. 'Junior wasn't so way-out when he tried to kill you before you even reached Endel. Maybe he knows his brother-in-law better than we think. The very obvious fact this last weekend that but for June's existence Robert might have been very happy to settle his problems in a very different way can't have given his wife much sleep. It must have put a real keen edge on her desire to get on with the job as originally scheduled.'

I said, 'You're making me want to crawl under a stone.'

'I'm not doing it for kicks. You want the picture, you can have it, warts and all.'

'I know.' I avoided his eyes. 'If Robert did kill Dolly, why did June tell me it was you?'

'When chucking dirt any extra dirt comes in handy. Tell me, apart from slugging bitches to death, what other forms did my derangement take?'

I told him the truth. I didn't enjoy it, either.

He said, 'If you only swallowed half, you were a bloody fool to let me into the mini.'

'I was too confused then to know what I'd swallowed.'

'How about now?'

'You've straightened me out on so much. Can't you finish the job?'

'Not tonight, Josephine. Not tonight.'

I flushed. 'I meant about your accident at work.'

'You want me to say I didn't cause it or kill my girl-friend. I could, but why should you believe me? I saved my own life as well as yours.'

'It's not only that. Was she your girl-friend?'

'No. Though I'd one at the time.'

'What's happened to her.'

'We were waiting for her divorce to come through. She didn't dig hospital visiting.' He smiled quickly and self-derisively. 'She's nothing against medicine. She's married a surgeon.'

'They knew about her?'

'A bit. That night June was ginned up she started making with the old "what you need is a wife" and being half-stoned myself I let the bit out. We had a great maudlin scene that ended with my spending the night in Endel. Like all clever liars, they kept as close to the truth as they dared.'

I said, 'I'm sorry.'

'I'd be the hell of a bloody liar if I said I was, now. I was damned upset about that other girl. She was a sweet kid and engaged to the man who died with her. He was a good man. I'll never get a better assistant.'

'You were in charge?'

'My department. My responsibility.'

167

'But were you in charge at the time?'

He took time to answer and when he did seemed to be dragging out his words. 'Technically, yes, even though I was off shift. They rang me when they suspected something was wrong. I could explain what, but I can't as I'm not allowed to. I'll tell you the part I can.' He drew in a long breath. 'I drove back to the office. I was in my own office taking off my coat when it went up. I hadn't time to talk to either or even get on my protective clobber. After the woomf my office was a sheet of flame. There was another woomf and the blast bunged me through the glass skylight. I landed on a roof with what remained of my clothes on fire and my glasses unbroken. The lads who had to pick up the pieces were hellish tickled by my glasses. They were even more bucked to have a live and only partially roasted guinea-pig to work on.' He broke off. 'Ever seen a radiation burn?'

'Aren't yours?'

'No. They should've been. I should've been fried to a crisp. I wasn't. The blast must've saved me. I just got burnt. Now I've healed the medics tell me – and have they tested! – I'm the lad I've always known and loved. I've not bothered to prove that since they let me out of hospital, but any time you want proof, just ask. Any time that is,' he added, 'that you want it, but not because you think it'll pay off your bill or help you shed your guilt-complex about me. You carry your own complexes, love, and I'll carry mine.' He looked at me over his glasses. 'Don't kid yourself you'll ever fool me on that one. I may be fool enough to have fallen for you so hard despite your initial reaction to me. I know very well that right now I could have you for the taking and you might even enjoy it. But I don't take calculated risks in bed and I've taken enough of those out of bed to recognize the smell even in the dark. You ever try one on me and you'll find yourself hitting the floor and I won't pick you up.'

'I'll bear that in mind.'

'You do that, Rose.' He breathed as if running. 'Having cleared that lot, let's get down to the larder and see what tins I've there. Now you've rested, we must eat something, then set course for St Martin's and the nearest cop.'

I got off the bed. 'Must we eat? Can't we get it over?'

'Not without food. It's a long walk and the mist's thick as hell. I'm not carrying you if you faint from hunger, and the cops'll listen that much better if we don't breathe whisky fumes. Come and give me a hand. Careful on the stairs in the dark.' He shut the bedroom door and the darkness enveloped us. 'I haven't covered the larder window. We'll grab the tins and bring 'em up for inspection.'

The larder was a slit of a room off the kitchen. I groped after him. My hand was on his shoulder when I felt him stiffen. 'David, what is it?'

'Quiet!' he breathed. 'Listen!'

I heard the sound then. 'Someone's outside!'

'Coming round from the front door. Wait here.' He vanished, then was back and pushing a poker into my hand. 'Don't use this unless you have to as it's heavy enough to crack any skull. Solid iron.'

The metal was cold as my hand. 'What about you?'

'Prefer my hands free.'

The steps had reached the back door. David pushed me into the larder. 'You're dead. Stay in here,' he whispered closing the door. I heard someone outside shaking the back door and then nearly laughed outright in relief as I recognized Murdo's voice cursing. His voice was so slurred and his accent so strong that I didn't catch one word clearly, but that broad Scottish flow was unmistakable.

David unlocked the door, drew back the bolts. 'Watch it, Murdo, or you'll fall back in a dyke! Come on in. Where's the estate?'

'Is it you, Mr Lofthouse? Och, away, mon, am I glad to see you! I'd leave the estate away up at St Martin's. The mist's that thick I couldn'a drive a wee bittie more, so I'd to walk – have ye no light in here?'

169

'Get out of the road and let me shut that door.' The back door slammed. I emerged from the larder as David lit a candle. The kitchen was full of mist and flickering shadows and Murdo swaying against the sink. Suddenly, he saw me and let out a high-pitched scream of terror. 'Yon's an apparition! Get away fra' me!' He flung himself on David, knocking the candle out of David's hand. It sizzled out on the wet floor. 'Did ye no' see it, Mr Lofthouse? Yon terrible apparition?'

David didn't pick up the candle. In the dark his voice was tight and hard. 'What are you talking about, lad?'

'Ye didn'a see it? The poor lassie that's been dead in the water these last two hours? Aye, mon, dead! The mini went down in the water. I heard them up the house! I heard them!'

'Mr and Mrs Endel and a lad?'

'Aye, the three – I heard them – all talking – when I was away into the hall to tell them I was back and to see to the fires, ye'll ken.'

'They told you the young lady had been drowned?' Murdo did not answer. 'Did they?' demanded David.

I stood still against the larder door, waiting.

'Och, mon, they didn'a ken I was there! I was that upset, I'd the urge for a wee dram – yon apparition – ye didn'a observe it?'

'No. Stop gibbering, lad, and talk sense! From your breath, you had that wee dram. Where'd you get it? Endel's wine cellar?'

'I'd to go down for more logs – it was no more than a wee drappie – and as I didn'a care for the lights I'd to take a wee look at the machine, ye'll ken. I'd a look' – he was gasping – 'and I was away out of the house fast!'

'Why?' David snapped out the word.

'I'm telling ye, mon! I'm telling ye! Had I put ma hand to the wee switch I'd be a dead mon!'

'Which switch is live?'

'Och, Mr Lofthouse, ye'll no' credit this, but there's no'

170

a switch in that machine it'll be safe to touch the whiles! It's all live!'

'Murdo, how many wee drams have you knocked back tonight?'

'Maybe I've had a drappie too much, but it's no' the whisky, Mr Lofthouse!' Murdo was nearly weeping. 'I ken well what I saw and what I heard. I heard them say the poor lassie was dead and heard them laughing! Mon, it was a terrible experience and yon apparition's returned to haunt me for not hasting back after her and waiting in the pub for the parcel that didn'a arrive! But had I touched that wee Monster, I'd now be dead ma'sel! I'm telling ye, it's been set wrong!'

'I believe you, though you're wrong about one thing. The young lady's not dead. She got out of the water.' David struck a match and lit another candle. 'Come closer, Rose. Let him touch you.'

The shock was too much for Murdo. David caught his sagging body before it hit the stone floor. He carried him into the living-room, laid him on the sofa as I stood by with another lighted candle. 'Put that thing out now, Rose.' He brushed past me in the dark and went upstairs. When he came down with two blankets he said he had turned off all the heaters and the lamp. 'Murdo may grill in his time, but we don't have to bring that time forward. I'll dump these blankets on him and on past showing he'll be out cold for an hour or so. Look what I've found.' He switched a torch on and off. 'I forgot I had it here. Coming?'

'Endel, or St Martin's?'

'A good question. You answer it.'

I was hollow with fear. 'St Martin's 'd be safer.'

'For us.'

I caught my breath. 'You think the Monster's set wrong, intentionally?'

'Don't you?'

'Yes. How long'll it take us to get to St Martin's?'

'Hour. Maybe more. Not less.'

'And another hour for someone to get out as it's too thick to drive?'

'Plus the time for explanations.'

'Yes.' I didn't know what had happened to my adrenalin. Perhaps I had used it all up getting out of the water. 'But you keep saying Robert won't take unnecessary risks. Won't two fatal accidents in one night be that?'

'Don't forget that right fly boy Junior, or that there's nothing like over-confidence plus alcohol for making anyone take risks. And there is our June.'

'I know. Have to be Endel. June may be a phoney and've helped try and kill me, but I'm beginning to wonder if she's ever any idea what she's doing. You heard her fussing about her mini! She seemed to have forgotten I was supposed to be in it.'

'Maybe she had. Maybe it was the only way she could go through with it. Maybe it was just a good act.'

'You think it was an act?'

'I personally think she's nutty as a fruit cake, but I'm no psychiatrist. I may be wrong. We may be the right nuts to consider moving in on 'em again. Still, we've one ace. They think you're dead. Think what that did to Murdo's much less guilty conscience.'

'I wish I could believe they'll swoon at the sight of me. Oh, well. Let's get it over.' I went into the kitchen and felt the cold water on the floor soaking through the ski socks I was wearing. 'I wish I'd my shoes.'

'That could be an advantage.' He removed the aged leather sandals he had found somewhere. 'No footsteps, now.'

'That won't stop the geese shouting.'

'Nor it will.' He opened the back door. 'Still black as pitch, but it doesn't smell of cheese.'

I recognized his source absently. 'I never liked Jorrocks.'

'Anti-blood sports?'

'Yes.'

'You could have fooled me.' He took my hand and

172

guided me along the path round the cottage. 'If you fall into the bloody dyke again,' he said, 'I'm not rescuing you. I'm going to sit down on the bank and cry.'

CHAPTER FIFTEEN

The geese scented us before we saw the house. The mist distorted their squarks to plaintive human wails. We heard a window opening and froze.

'That you, Murdo?' Robert's shout was nearer than I had expected.

As we were not approaching their lean-to, the geese were getting bored. The gander gave out a final honk and there was silence.

'Murdo?' shouted Robert again. 'Did you have to ditch the estate and walk?'

Not even the gander answered. A minute, or an hour later, we heard the window closing.

David pressed his lips against my ear. 'What was your rating at Grandmother's Footsteps?'

'Low. I always giggled. You?' I murmured.

'Olympic Class.' He gripped my elbow. 'Thisaway.'

We were a few feet from the front steps before we saw the outline of the house through the mist. The Monster had stopped and they were using candles in the sitting-room. The hall and upstairs front windows were dark.

David guided me away from the house, across the yard and into the first of the empty garages. The geese squarked, occasionally. He said, 'Let's pray they think we're rats,' and with his torch briefly illuminated a stack of empty crates and sacks piled against the back wall. 'There's a door back here that leads into an old tunnel to the cellars that runs under the yard. Murdo showed it me once when the Endels were out. Obviously an old escape route when smuggling was your family's pet hobby. Here we are!'

We were not, as the door though unlocked was bolted on the inside. David said, 'Have to be via the kitchen. Soon as we're sure where they all are, we'll nip down. I want to look at the Monster before we try for the phone – if it's working – as that machine's such a mass of contradictions there's just a chance the fault or faults could be genuine. We've enough to tell the cops without spoiling the effect with false alarms.'

'I thought you believed Murdo?'

'I do. But having that nasty suspicious streak – and so forth.' He replaced the crates as before. 'They'll shove over easily if we have to make a hasty exit.'

'David, if the phone's useless, what exactly do we do?'

'You could stay here while I find out.'

'That's a lousy idea!'

'I can think of worse.'

'Forget 'em. I'm your ace.'

'And you natter too much when you're scared.' He put a finger on my lips then ran it slowly across my face. 'Take it easy, honey. The U.S. Cavalry won't let us down.'

I smiled reluctantly and felt for his hand. He locked his fingers through mine and we crossed the yard and soundlessly went in through the kitchen door.

The kitchen was in darkness. The passage leading past it to the hall was lit dimly by a small hurricane lamp on the top step of the cellar stairs. The door to the stairs was open. I mouthed 'Looks genuine.' David shrugged and moved ahead to the swing door. He held it a little open and immediately we heard voices in the sitting-room. We waited, listening.

The hall fire was out and the sitting-room door shut, but we heard them clearly as they were really living. June had started giggling; Adrian sounded nearly as drunk as Murdo before he passed out; Robert's voice was louder than usual and slightly bellicose. They were discussing Adrian's return to London.

'I'd much sooner go tonight, Rob, even if it means a

174

long walk. My knee doesn't hurt now June's restrapped it. I hate early rising!'

'Too bad,' retorted Robert, 'as you'll just have to put up with it, mate! Have another drink!'

A bottle clinked against glasses. Adrian said, 'Surely, this mist'll lift soon?'

'More likely it'll last all night. You try walking anywhere and you'll end up under water, too! Murdo's obviously stuck out in it, but even if he does make it back with the estate, I'm not driving anywhere until it clears or it's daylight. If Murdo's back by dawn,' went on Robert, 'I'll run you in to Astead via St Martin's. If he doesn't show up, I'll walk over to knock up Bill Parker soon as it's light, tell him I couldn't contact him earlier as our phone's busted and get him to come back with me and represent the law when I start dredging up the mini. I'll ring for a taxi for you from St Martin's. Remind me to wear a black tie. Hey, June! Wakey wakey! You can't sleep yet. Let's have your glass and then I'll get another bottle.'

June giggled, 'I'm tiddley! Darling, if you're going down, can you look at the Monster? I've plugged in all the upstairs fires like you said, but if we don't have some heat in them soon, the bedrooms'll be icy!'

Adrian said, 'Pity your emergency's run out.'

'Bound to run out as we've used up the batteries. All right!' Robert sounded as if getting off the sofa. 'Probably the sod's still too hot to touch as that always happens when the main fuses blow, but I'll take a look. We need more wine, anyway.'

David let the swing door fall shut and pushed me into the pantry. He stood in front of me behind the half-open pantry door. Robert went by humming to himself and his foosteps clattered on the stone stair. I waited till they faded. 'Maybe we're right out?'

'Maybe. I still want a gander below.'

Robert took his time. Minutes dragged by. June and Adrian were talking but now too quietly for us to hear their conversation. Robert returned, still humming. The hall door swung behind him and he was in the hall when his steps paused. 'Hell! I've left the wine below! Make yourself useful, Adrian,' he called, 'and get it for me. I've been up and down those stairs enough for one night!' The sitting-room door opened. 'That fire needs more logs. I'll get 'em in from the chest out here while you nip down for that bottle. It's on the floor by the machine, but though I think it's all off, as parts are still too hot to touch I can't swear it's safe, so for God's sake don't touch anything but the bottle!'

'Oh, my word, no, Adrian!' squeaked June. 'You be careful! Want any help, Robert, darling?'

'You could bring out one of those candleholders and give me some light, Junie.'

'I'll do that for you, Rob.' Adrian's voice was very slurred. 'My dears! What are these things made of? Cast iron?'

'Cast iron, indeed! My lovely pewter candleholders! Give it me, Adrian,' insisted June, 'and you get off to the cellars!'

Robert said, 'Don't break that bloody bottle or your neck on the cellar stairs!'

'Trust me to look out for myself!' Adrian laughed foolishly. He knocked into the passage wall twice and stumbled on the stairs even though he had taken the lamp with him, blacking out the pantry and passage.

'Down, now! Bolt or lock the door if possible after us,' murmured David, vanishing. I groped after him with my heart making such a noise that I felt it must be heard in the hall. Luckily, Robert dropped some logs. I heard June's petulant, 'Darling you'll scratch the floor!' as I quietly closed the cellar door. It had no key, but one bolt on the inside which I shot. I could still hear June scampering round the hall picking up logs and nagging Robert to remember the floor polish. She was not doing much good.

Another load of logs rolled across the floor.

The stairs were steep, slippery and winding. I took them slowly in the dark and was still on them when I heard a key turning in the door I had just bolted. I slithered the rest of the way and the dank blackness was as chilling as the sound of that key turning. I could see nothing. Then, somewhere ahead, a torch flicked on and off. I made for the spot. I had to tell David someone above had locked Adrian in and I must NOT think of rats. If I saw one, David and everyone else in Endel was going to hear me.

I speeded up and ran into a wall. Jerking back, I discovered I had come to the end of a passage and there was another running at right angles to it. David was creeping towards an open doorway on the left. Suddenly he ran forward and was outlined in amber light. 'Get away from that machine, lad!' he warned urgently.

'What the hell're you doing here?' Adrian held up the lamp as I reached David's side. 'My God! Rose!' He backed in a horror that was even more acute than Murdo's and flung the lamp directly at me. It didn't hit me as David knocked me out of the way. The lamp sailed over my shoulder and crashed on the wall behind me. The glass shattered and the automatic safety mechanism put out the flame before the spilt oil could explode.

The beam of David's torch picked out the wine bottle on the floor. 'Come away from that machine and leave that bloody bottle alone! It's probably live!'

'Adrian! Do what he says!' I urged.

Either Adrian was too drunk to understand, or he merely understood I was no ghost. He grabbed at the bottle as if to hurl it after the lamp. The blinding blue flash was instantaneous and instantly followed by a sharp crack. I had a nightmarish glimpse of Adrian's illuminated body being jerked in the air as David pulled me away from the doorway and we toppled in a heap on to the passage floor. After the second blue flash, he was lying on top of me. The

177

second report was louder than the first. and made the floor vibrate. There was one more flash, one more crack, and then silence.

David raised his head. 'There can't now be a fuse left to blow – Christ!' He flattened himself as there was a different and absolutely thunderous crack somewhere overhead. 'That's no fuse!'

'What was it?'

'Don't ask me.' He rolled off me and helped me up. 'Right now, not even a Jehovah's Thunderbolt'ld surprise me.' He switched on his torch and inhaled quickly. 'You'll have to look,' he muttered, 'but take it easy as the poor lad's not pretty. Don't touch him or go a step nearer. I don't think there can be any current left, but if there is, though the poor devil's dead, he can still be live.'

Adrian lay in a queer and rigid curve, his body resting on his head and his heels. His open eyes were staring and his lips were drawn back from his teeth in a frozen grin. The wine bottle, still intact, had rolled on to its side.

I was sweating with nausea. 'I don't understand. That bottle isn't connected to anything.'

'It didn't have to be. Take a look at the floor under the machine and the thing itself. All soaking wet.' The narrow beam of light moved over the great machine and the flagstones beneath. 'So simple. That bottle was standing on a wet patch. He probably shoved it in a bucket of water to make quite sure. Nothing'ld dry out on a night like this. As the current was on, anyone touching the bottle would take the lot.'

I had to look away or vomit. 'Can't we do anything for him? You're sure he's dead?'

'Looks it. Kiss of life might work. Stay here.' Very carefully he began edging his way round the machine. 'I think I can reach the master switch. It must be safe or Robert couldn't have set this up.'

'Careful! Be careful!'

'What the hell do you think I'm being?' He pushed up

178

a lever, then pulled out a row of plugs. I did not even breathe out when he said the machine was dead. I waited until I helped him lift Adrian's body into the passage as we needed more room. He said, 'I don't think we've a hope in hell, but we'll try it.'

We both tried to breathe life into Adrian. We did not succeed. We were so busy trying that we forgot everything else until the faint rumbling started above.

I sat back on my heels. 'What's going on up there?'

He brushed his mouth with the back of his hand. 'We're under the drawing-room here. Sounded higher than that. As we're not doing any good, we'd better get up and find out.'

'We can't.' I told him about that key turning. 'Think it was Robert and he saw us?'

'More likely he doesn't want June to see this poor bastard. That must be why he's not come down to investigate results. Probably he's told her Adrian's locked himself down accidentally. He's a right one for accidents!'

'He won't get away with this! We saw it!'

'We did,' he said wearily, 'but we also saw he was stoned and heard Robert warning him to be very careful. So did June and under oath we'll have to say so. I doubt even a manslaughter'll stick. Death by misadventure.'

'You really believe that?'

A sudden fall of dust enveloped us before he could answer. His glasses kept some of it out of his eyes, but momentarily I was blinded. Before I could see properly the rumbling grew louder and the dust began to fall continuously.

'Come on!' David hauled me to my feet and down the passage. 'Out, fast! I don't know what's going on and we're not hanging around to be buried alive while we find out. We'll take the tunnel under the yard. That builder Yates wasn't kidding when he said there's a limit to how much these foundations can take.'

The dank air grew thicker and thicker with the dislodged dust of centuries. The tremor of the passage walls and the ground under our feet was slight but constant. The cellars were honeycombed with passages and we took three wrong turnings before we found the one running away from the house. It was a tunnel about four feet wide and five high. The walls and roof were bricked and supported by thick wooden props. The air was much less dusty but more foul.

'Right set of dwarfs, your ancestors,' grunted David, as we stumbled on, doubled-up. 'Good!' His torch beam fell on cracked stone steps leading up to a woodlice-encrusted wooden door. The huge bolt was very old but it had been newly oiled and opened easily. 'Someone else's had the same bright idea. Wait,' he said, 'I'll shift those crates, but as I don't want to advertise our presence by knocking them over, I'll have to go slow.'

I looked back at the dark tunnel and thought of Adrian and shivered. 'Why should Robert want a quick getaway? Or do you think he intends bringing Adrian out this way so June won't see?'

'No point in that. It was another accident. When he brings in the law tomorrow, he'll want the law to see just how it happened.'

'What about all that water?'

'A couple of minutes with a good blow-lamp'll turn that into normal dampness.'

'Maybe that's why he oiled the bolt?'

'Maybe.'

'You don't sound very certain.'

'I'm not. I'm not even certain this flaming house is going to be standing by morning. Try this for size.'

I squeezed through behind the crates. He followed me, then pushed them back. 'That rumbling's stopped.'

We went out of the garage and stood in the shadow by the wall. The mist was beginning to lift. The outline of Endel was clear and solid. I said, 'Whatever was shaken up must've settled. It's so quiet.'

'Too bloody quiet.'

'Isn't that a good sign? As far as the house is concerned?'

'Not necessarily. Didn't they teach you about stresses and strains when you did physics at school?'

'Didn't do physics. Not even sure what it is.'

'The science of how things work. Tell you all – some other time. Got your breath back?'

'More or less. Why? What do we do now?'

He said, 'You walk down to End, chuck a bucket of water over Murdo, get him to take you to St Martin's and tell the cops to get a move on and bring an ambulance.'

'I'm not leaving you! Aren't I your ace?'

'Right now, you're the Ace of Spades. Death card, in case you don't know. If Robert sees you, as he's now in too deep for any remnants of caution, God help us all – including June. Alone, as the mist's lifting, I should be able to stall things while you get help here. We haven't been able to prevent one murder, so let's not make a bloody habit of it—' He stopped speaking. June was calling.

She was somewhere in the house. 'Coo-eee! Coo-eee! Adrian! Adrian! You can come up now! It's quite safe!' She hammered on a door. 'Come up this way! Coo-eee! You don't have to go out to the garage! You can unbolt this and come up this way!'

I clutched David's arm. 'The door I bolted?'

'Guess so. Quiet!'

June was shouting more loudly, but her shouts were calm and affectionate. She might have been shouting 'lunch is ready!'

'David, where's Robert?'

'How'd I know? God Almighty!' Endel had suddenly quivered. A stream of roof tiles hit the yard like hailstones. 'You see it, Rose? It wasn't the crack in my glasses?'

'No. I saw it. There – again!' June was now silent. 'They must feel it inside!'

'You'd think so. Get Murdo. The cops'll have to wait,

but I want another man. Sober him up, fast!'

'You're not going into Endel now? Ace of Spades or not, I'm coming with you!'

He said almost gently, 'Try it and I'll belt you one that'll have you colder than Murdo – and much help you'll be then.'

I didn't argue. 'All right,' I lied.

He went in through the kitchen again. I gave him about a minute. The geese were shouting full blast and the roof tiles were cascading down.

In the kitchen it was gently raining plaster and a row of saucepans slid languidly off a shelf. I had never been in an earthquake, but the sensation was exactly as I imagined an earthquake would provide. The whole house seemed to be swaying, but not violently. It was a very slight sway, but it was enough to be terrifying.

David was calling. 'June? Robert? Is anyone home?'

No one answered him.

He came out of the sitting-room, the lighted torch in his hand, as I reached the swing door. He did not see me as I waited watching through a chink as we had done earlier. The sitting-room candles had gone out and I had a glimpse of the glowing white ash in the hearth before the door slammed itself behind him. I was looking at him, so I saw his outline stiffen before I saw the reason. He moved forward as if the hall floor were hot. 'Hallo, June. It's David.' His voice was carefully casual. 'I came back for some stuff I'd left in End and noticed your lights were out. Monster packed it in, again?' The torch beam moved. 'What's up with Robert? Been took queer?'

June was sitting on the log-chest, her hands folded in her lap. Robert lay face downwards on the floor at her feet. She blinked in the light, but did not move. 'There was a sort of bang and it made me drop the candleholder and the candles went out. Have you any matches, David?'

CHAPTER SIXTEEN

David picked up the candleholder, replaced and lit the candles. The flickering light did not reach to the corners of the long hall. I slid through the swing door and moved closer, keeping in the shadows. As the hall was the strongest part of the house, it was much steadier than the kitchen. The pewter trays and plates on the walls jangled softly, but only one had fallen. It lay on the floor near Robert.

June said placidly, 'Poor Robert. That bang knocked that tray off the wall and fell on his head as he was getting logs. I'm waiting for my brother to help move him. I'm not allowed to lift. It's such a heavy tray. The edge is dented. Can it be straightened?'

'I expect so.' I saw David look at her quickly and then look upwards as he crouched by Robert. 'Must've been some bang. There was a new and icily guarded note in his voice. 'It may not have done this house much good. I think you should go outside, June. I'll see to Robert for you.' Swiftly, he opened the front door. 'Come along, June. The mist's nearly gone.'

'Good. I hate mists!' She got off the chest, but instead of going outside walked round to pick up the fallen tray. 'If this edge can't be straightened, it'll ruin the set and Robert'll be so cross.' She spoke as if he were up at the farm and not on the floor at her feet.

'It'll be put right,' David was very gentle. 'Come on, love. Have some fresh air.'

'Not now, David. I've to wait for my brother!'

'Why not wait for him by the mounting block?' The hall had now begun to sway very slightly. 'June, I don't think you quite understand. That bang could've upset the foundations and if so, that could be a little dangerous.

You come along, or I'll have to carry you out.'

'No!' She backed from him. 'It's you who doesn't understand! I can't leave Robert! He's hurt! I must wait for Adrian to help him to bed! You're not to touch him!'

I stepped forward. 'June, he must and you must do as David says! We must all get out in the open.'

She neither backed in horror nor fainted. She just looked at me blankly as David spun round. 'You stupid bitch! Get out – take her with you – and stay out! Don't you realize this bloody roof's about to come in?' He stepped towards me, threateningly. 'I wasn't kidding when I said I'd belt you one. Take your pick – but fast!'

I said, 'It's all right, David. We're leaving. Come with me, June.'

She seemed neither to hear nor see me. She said in a vague squeak, 'I have to stay with Robert.'

'Christ!' muttered David. 'I'll get him out right now!' He stooped over Robert's limp body and as he did so June swung the heavy tray above her head and held it poised in both hands. I shouted a warning to David as I dived at her. She had aimed to get the back of his bent head with the edge of the tray. Had she hit him as she intended, probably she would have killed him. As it was, she hit him with the flat of the tray and hard enough to knock him genuinely unconscious. He slumped over Robert and the tray clattered across the hall. June gave me a push that sent me staggering backwards, then picked up the tray and sat with it on the log-box. She ignored the men on the floor as she polished the tray with her skirt. She looked at me and in the candlelight her eyes were blank as blue marbles.

I didn't know if it were possible to be too frightened for fear, but that was what seemed to have happened to me. I had to swallow several times before I could speak. 'David was only trying to help, June.'

'He shouldn't have touched Robert. He should've waited for Adrian, like I said! He shouldn't interfere so much!

184

And, anyway, he shouldn't have said he'd hit you! Men shouldn't hit women. It's not fair. They've got stronger muscles and they only do it because they think they can't be hurt back! They can!' She giggled. 'Look at them now!'

I knelt by David, watching her warily. He had not been wearing his glasses. I did not know when he had taken them off but just thanked God he had. He was breathing and his face was warm.

June said, 'I hate men who hit women. I always want to hit them. I'd like to kill them. Wouldn't you?'

'Perhaps I've been lucky. No one's ever hit me.'

'Oh, my word, you are lucky!' She shivered violently. 'You bet you are!'

I managed to ease David off Robert. Robert's face was icy. I held my hand in front of his nose and mouth. No breath. 'June, has some man hit you?' My voice shook, but I doubted she noticed. 'Was he your stepfather?'

She gave a kind of agonised squeal, put down the tray on the chest beside her and covered her face with her hands. 'I won't talk about him – I won't – I won't – you mustn't make me' – she was weeping hysterically – 'you mustn't make me remember – I won't remember – he used to take off his belt – it had a buckle – mother didn't stop him – she said he was my new dad – I won't talk about him—'

I had to go over to her. I put my arms round her shoulders and she flopped against me, still weeping. 'You don't have to talk about him, June. It's all over, long ago.'

She could not stop. 'I told Robert – just once – and he promised he'd never hit me – never – but tonight – he got mad at me when I said he was scratching the floor. He was scratching the floor,' she wailed pathetically, 'and it's such a lovely floor! He turned round with his hand up – so I had to hit him. I used the candleholder.' Her tears stopped like a tap turning off. 'He fell down.'

'It wasn't your fault. You didn't mean to hurt him. I suppose the tray then fell on him?'

'It didn't hit him when it fell.' She let go of me, mopped her eyes and polished the tray again. 'I hit him with it. I had to hit him again. Can this be straightened?'

'I'm sure it can.' I was calm because I had to be. I had no idea how I managed it. 'Can you now give me a hand with David? He wouldn't really have hit me. He's too kind. He just likes talking nonsense.'

'It's not nonsense! He killed Dolly! Robert said so! Anyway, I'm not allowed to lift. The doctor said I mustn't. I had an operation. Did you know?'

'You've never told me.' I glanced upwards, fearfully. Much longer and we would all be buried alive. If I tried to drag her out she would almost certainly get away from me as she was stronger than myself. If I tried to knock her out, unless I succeeded straight off, she might very likely kill me. That wouldn't help either her or David.

She said, 'Robert told me not to talk about my fall or losing my baby. Robert said that way I'd forget. Sometimes, I did. Sometimes I thought I was having a baby. Isn't that funny?'

'I've heard it can happen.' Keeping my back away from her I started lugging David by the shoulders towards the front door. 'I'm very sorry you lost your baby.'

'Grandfather said he was sorry. Robert said he couldn't help stumbling against me as he was so old. Do you know what I did?'

'No.'

She laughed girlishly. 'I said I was sorry when I held the pillow over his horrid old face. Robert doesn't know that! You won't tell him, will you? Promise?'

'I promise.' I wanted to stop for breath, to push the dust out of my eyes and to weep. There was no time. 'June, hold the front door for me. It may blow shut.'

She didn't move. She didn't hear me. She didn't know whom I was or what was happening to Endel. She was a broken mind in a strong body. She was talking on, mechanically, 'Robert's so clever, but he's never understood about the baby. He said I'd feel different about it after my operation. I didn't. I wanted my baby. Adrian understood. Adrian's not clever like Robert, but he always understands things. Adrian's my brother, you see, and when he was a little kid I used to play with him and pretend he was my baby. I still do – so I have to look after him. Have you met Adrian?'

'You've never introduced me.' I had reached the front door. I heaved David out and let him slither down the steps. As he was so limp, I hoped it would not hurt him too much. I looked at him briefly, then went back in. 'June. Come with me. Please.

'I want to tell you something first.' She patted the chest. 'Sit down.'

I hesitated, then sat. 'What, June?'

'Adrian's just a teeny bit frightened of Robert. I've thought he was before though he's always pretended he wasn't, but tonight, he told me.'

'Was there some special reason? Tonight?'

'I don't know – I think so – I forget. But we had a sort of party, you see, and we all got a bit tight – it was good fun – until Adrian told me when Robert wasn't there that he was rather frightened and wanted to go back to London. But Robert didn't want him to go – at least not until tomorrow. So I had a brainwave! I told him to make any excuse and go down to the cellars and then go out by the old door that opens into the garage. We don't often use that door, but I knew the bolt wouldn't stick as Robert only oiled it – I forget when – but it was when we had an awful gale. I forget why he oiled it – perhaps he didn't tell me. Perhaps he did. I keep sort of forgetting things. Do you?'

'Often. June – tell me the rest outside.'

She ignored that. 'It was so lucky! Adrian didn't have to make any excuse because Robert asked him to go down for a bottle of wine. Adrian went down. I didn't think he'd bother about the bottle – though he does like wine – not that he drinks too much! Anyway, when he was getting the bottle – Robert said it was by the Monster – and Adrian must've done something wrong as I heard the Monster making an awful noise just after he went down, so I expect he thought he'd have another drink first and accidentally pushed the wrong switch. Robert didn't hear as I think I must've knocked him out when I hit him with the candle-holder, but after that huge bang made the tray fall, he began to wake up. So I had to hit him again. He gets so cross when people upset his Monster, and I couldn't let him get cross with Adrian, could I?'

'No. Now, June—'

'Do stop interrupting! It's not polite! I haven't finished! I'll have to tell you as you must stick to my story, too. It's quite clever.' She put down the tray and smoothed her skirt. 'I was going to tell Robert the Monster went wrong by itself – it does that sometimes – and he got hurt because that tray fell – but now,' she added triumphantly, 'I'm going to say it was David! I'll say that's why I hit David. Isn't it lucky he came back?'

'Very.'

'I was going to tell Adrian to back up my first idea – that's one reason why I waited here for him. I wanted him to carry Robert up to bed before he goes back to London. Robert'll be so pleased with him for that he won't mind when I say Adrian's gone. I think I'll wait to say that until tomorrow. He may have a headache tonight and men get so bad-tempered when they're not well. And Adrian's going to be so pleased to have David as such a perfect excuse!' She looked round. 'Where is David?'

'Outside.' I stood up. 'Come and look.'

'Not till Adrian comes. I don't know where he's got to. I've called and called. I wish he hadn't bolted the cellar door. I've tried to get down to find him. I couldn't and it's no use my trying the garage as that's bolted on the other side. He must've heard me calling – unless he's sleep-

188

ing off all that wine he had. He was rather drunk. But he wouldn't have gone back to London without his suitcase. He put it on a shelf in the boot-room this afternoon when he arrived and it's still there. I found it after trying the cellar door.'

'Perhaps the place to look is the garage?'

'Do you think so? But if we leave Robert he may wake up again.'

I said tautly, 'I don't think he will just yet. And you want to find Adrian.'

'Yes, I must. He's only a kid – sometimes he does quite silly things. I have to look after him.'

I took her hand. 'Let's go, June.'

We were on the front steps when she suddenly wrenched away her hand and ran back up. 'I've forgotten my tray! Adrian'll straighten it – he's so good with his hands!'

She was in the hall and I had reached the front doorway when the main beam of the house finally snapped. David had staggered to his feet. He lunged for my legs in a rugger tackle and we fell down the front steps together as the roof caved in. It sounded as if the whole world was breaking up.

It was a very long time before the noise died away, the dust cloud settled and the geese had shouted themselves hoarse. By then, David and I were sitting on the grass verge on the far side of the drive. Later, neither of us remembered how we got there. It was about the only thing that happened that night that I didn't remember.

CHAPTER SEVENTEEN

The Chief Constable had been born on the marsh and had known my father and uncle as boys. He had been attending a police dinner in Astead when P.C. Parker rang his duty sergeant. The Chief Constable drove out to see for himself. Throughout our first meeting he addressed me as 'madam'. After the triple inquest he introduced me to his wife as 'Rosser's girl'. His wife and Mrs Wenden were second cousins. All three and half the marsh came to the funeral. It rained all that day and one of the television outside broadcasting vans had to be dragged out of the mud by an Endel tractor driven by the farm foreman who was now acting-manager. David recognized the tractor as the one that had caused our skid.

The coroner returned the same verdict on them all. Death by misadventure.

Mr Yates, in his Sunday suit and a black tie, was still torn between sympathy and irritation when we shook hands after the funeral. 'As I said at the inquest, madam, if only he'd paid me more heed, it wouldn't have happened. Too like your grandad, I reckon. Old Mr Endel wouldn't be told, neither. There it is.'

David and I were staying with the Wendens at Shepland. David left for Coventry on the day after the funeral. I drove with him as far as Astead. I had a luncheon appointment with the Endel's family solicitor and after lunch we were meeting the insurance assessor on the site. The solicitor was driving me to Midstreet and later back to Shepland.

David did not talk much during the drive to Astead. Recently, we had had to do so much talking to other people that when alone together, more often than not, we were silent.

He drew up in a lay-by just outside Astead. He said, 'There's something you'd better know, Rose. I'm not going to ask you to marry me now and I never will.'

'Thanks,' I said, 'for putting me straight.'

'Belt up,' he said, 'I haven't finished. I won't ask you, but that doesn't mean I don't want to marry you or won't, if you ask me. And you needn't ask nicely.'

I smiled slightly. 'I'll bear that in mind.'

'You do that.' He removed his glasses and kissed me.

Then he replaced them, drove on and said no more until he dropped me at the solicitor's office. 'You don't have to want to marry me. You just have to want me around.'

'You'd settle for that?'

He hitched down his glasses and blinked thoughtfully. 'For you, love, anything. Take me up on that, sometime?'

'I may well do that, David. Thanks for the lift.'

He waved and drove off rather too quickly. I watched the back of his head through his car's rear window until he turned out of the High Street.

That was the last I saw of him for quite a while. Then I wrote him a letter and he wired back by return. We met in London on the evening of the day I had his wire. I was very early for our date. David was waiting when I got there.

A SELECTED LIST OF CORGI ROMANCE
FOR YOUR READING PLEASURE

ORDER FORM

All these books are available at your bookshop or newsagent, or can be ordered direct from the publisher. Just tick the titles you want and fill in the form below.

CORGI BOOKS, Cash Sales Department, P.O. Box 11, Falmouth, Cornwall.

Please send cheque or postal order, no currency.

U.K. Please allow 30p for the first book, 15p for the second book and 12p for each additional book ordered to a maximum charge of £1.29.

B.F.P.O. and Eire. Please allow 30p for the first book, 15p for the second book plus 12p per copy for the next seven books, thereafter 6p per book.

Overseas customers. Please allow 50p for the first book and 15p per copy for each additional book.

NAME (block letters) ●●

ADDRESS ●●●

●●●

While every effort is made to keep prices low, it is sometimes necessary to increase prices at short notice. Corgi books reserve the right to show new retail prices on covers which may differ from those previously advertised in the text or elsewhere.